Other books by Carolyn Brown

The Dove
The PMS Club
Trouble in Paradise
The Wager
That Way Again
Lily's White Lace
The Ivy Tree
The Yard Rose
All the Way from Texas
A Falling Star
Love Is

The Angels & Outlaws Historical Romance Series:

From Wine to Water
Walkin' On Clouds

The Black Swan Historical Romance Series:

From Thin Air
Pushin' Up Daisies
Come High Water

The Broken Roads Romance Series:

To Hope
To Dream
To Believe
To Trust
To Commit

The Drifters and Dreamers Romance Series:

Morning Glory
Sweet Tilly
Evening Star

A TRICK OF THE LIGHT

An Angels & Outlaws Historical Romance

A TRICK OF THE LIGHT

•

Carolyn Brown

AVALON BOOKS
NEW YORK

Published by Avalon Books,
an imprint of Thomas Bouregy & Co., Inc.
160 Madison Avenue, New York, NY 10016

Library of Congress Cataloging-in-Publication Data

Brown, Carolyn, 1948–
A Trick of the light : an angels & outlaws historical romance / Carolyn Brown.
p. cm.
ISBN 978-0-8034-7671-4 (acid-free paper)
I. Title.
PS3552.R685275T75 2011
813'.54—dc22

2011005562

PRINTED IN THE UNITED STATES OF AMERICA
ON ACID-FREE PAPER
BY RR DONNELLEY, BLOOMSBURG, PENNSYLVANIA

Chapter One

"I— I killed your father." Sally Duval gasped for air. Her hands were clammy and her voice weak. Her lips were a faint shade of blue, and the tips of her fingers were turning dusky. Her brown hair was spread out on the pillow like a dark halo around her pretty face, and her brown eyes searched Micah Burnet's face for forgiveness.

He leaned closer to his dying fiancée's lips. Surely he'd misunderstood her words. The cold wind he'd endured while racing his horse from his plantation to her aunt and uncle's must have impaired his hearing. A bandit had killed his father more than a year before. Shot him in the back and stole his horse. He and his brother, Isaac, and their cousin, Tyrell, had trailed the man all the way to San Antonio, Texas, only to arrive a day too late. The bandit had tried to rob a bank and had gotten killed in the process.

"What makes you think such a thing? You are delirious with fever. You don't know what you're talking about," Micah said.

She clasped his hands desperately. "Listen to me, Micah. I am dying, and I'm speaking the truth."

"Why would you think that you killed my father? He was shot for his horse, remember?" Micah argued.

Her breathing was shallow and her words barely audible. "I . . . was meeting another man on the sly out at the cabin. I had loved Frank since we were kids, but you were a better catch, so it was my last chance to be with Frank. Your father came out there unannounced and caught me asleep. Frank had left, but your father knew about him and me. He told me to get dressed and leave but that he was going to tell you what kind of woman I was."

Micah let go of her hands and straightened up, glad that no one else was in the room with them. The walls began to move toward him, and he felt as if he'd be trapped forever in that bedroom with Sally dying before his eyes.

Micah raked his fingertips through his dark hair. "I can't believe you'd do that."

She spoke in raspy tones, her eyes now nearly closed. "I shot him in the back. I was going to shoot his horse too, but a man rode by, and I gave it to him. He'd robbed a bank in Jackson and was on the run. Told me to ride away with him, and I almost did, but I needed to be there to console you for the death of your father."

She looked so frail lying in the bed with the covers up to her chin. On Sunday she'd been the very essence of life at the church social, and she'd been his future wife. Three days later she was dying and admitting a horrible crime.

Micah needed space and time. His heart had turned to a stone in his chest. His mind ran in circles as he thought back on the day he'd found his father shot through the heart and still warm up by the old cabin. He'd held Morris Burnet in his arms and begged him not to die, vowed he would find the man who'd shot him in the back and exact revenge. Now, a year later, those old wounds were reopened in Micah, and the horrid feeling of numbness encased inside a wall of anger had returned.

Sally's eyes opened slowly, and her fingers nervously fidgeted with the edge of the quilt. "I can't die with that on my conscience, Micah. I'm fond of you. We would have made a good couple."

He raked his fingers through his hair and looked at the pillow. He couldn't bring himself to actually look into her eyes. "You would have married me without telling me. Why are you telling me now?"

Her breathing was shallow and labored. "I promised God I'd confess on my deathbed if I didn't get caught. I . . . I hoped you'd die before me so I'd never have to tell you."

The doctor opened the door. "Mr. Burnet, I need to give her another dose of medicine."

"Forgive me," she gasped.

Those were Sally's last words as she took her final breath and let it out slowly.

Micah walked out of the room, down the stairs, and out the front door. He mounted his horse and rode off the Duval property with his head in a spin. An hour later he sat down on the very spot where he'd found his father.

Three weeks before, he'd asked Sally to marry him after courting her all winter. She'd been wearing his ring when he let go of her hands and left the room. He would have felt better if she'd taken her secret with her to the grave. He held his aching head with his big, callused hands and wished he'd never met the woman the year before, when she came to live with her aunt and uncle on the adjoining plantation.

Tempest Lavalle was restless when she awoke that morning at her sister Delia's home. She'd sent her maid, Dotty, away and dressed herself, braiding her long black curly hair into long ropes that she wrapped around her head. Delia had given birth the previous week to a healthy daughter she'd named Etta Ruth after both her mother and Tyrell's. Her other sister, Fairlee, was happily married to Tyrell's cousin, Isaac Burnet.

Delia and Tyrell Fannin's two-story house sat in one corner of River Bend, the Burnet and Fannin plantation. Micah and Isaac Burnet were brothers and had been raised in the house in the middle of the plantation. Tyrell was their cousin, and his parents had built on a corner of the land about a mile away. In the beginning there was only a single cabin on the land, at the far diagonal corner from Tyrell's house, and that's where Fairlee and Isaac were living while their new house was being built. That's where Tempest was headed that morning. The two-mile ride would exercise her horse and clear the antsy feeling from her heart.

"Maybe I'll go the long way," she said aloud as she grabbed a biscuit in the kitchen and went straight for the stables, where she saddled her horse. She started to ride the perimeter of the land but changed her mind and took the shorter route, straight as the arrow flew, from Tyrell's, diagonally across River Bend, to Micah's and then to the cabin. She kneed the horse and let him run full speed until she passed Micah's, and then she reined him in to a steady trot. Already she felt better. The sun teased the horizon, and the smell of breakfast cooking in the servants' quarters wafted across the land. It was going to be a glorious day. When she got home, she'd be in a much better mood than when she woke up.

Home. That had a strange ring to it. Home had always been in northern Louisiana, just over the border from Texas and near Bennet's Bluff. But now that her sisters had settled in Mississippi, and her parents, Captain Robert and Rosetta Lavalle, had both passed, she had a new home. The jury was still out on whether she was going to like it or not or whether she'd stay there permanently.

The morning air held the promise of spring—slightly nippy, but the sun would bring a nice warm afternoon. Minty green buds were popping out on the willow and elm trees. The pecans weren't ready to come out of hibernation, but then, they were always the laziest trees in the spring.

Her horse neighed at another animal not thirty feet away, and she pulled up the reins. No one should be out that early. Tyrell was an early riser, but even he had still been asleep when she left the house. She squinted in the dim morning light, and she could see a horse standing in the open with a man sitting on the ground nearby. Maybe he was hurt, or maybe it was a ruse. She was, after all, riding in the same place that Isaac and Micah's father was killed the year before.

She drew her rifle from the side of her saddle and rode on slowly. Was that Micah's horse?

"Micah?"

"Over here. What are you doing out this early? Is something wrong?"

She dismounted and tied her horse to a sapling. "Nothing is wrong. I just woke up early and couldn't sleep, so I went for a ride. What are *you* doing out so early?"

Micah didn't look up or answer. Of all the people in the entire world, Tempest Lavalle would have been his last choice to see that morning. He would rather have faced off with Lucifer than his brother's sister-in-law. Three Lavalle sisters had ridden for home with them out of San Antonio, Texas, the previous year. Delia, the eldest, married Tyrell and came on home to Greenville, Mississippi, with them. Then Fairlee, the next one in line, was about to make a big mistake and marry a rogue back in Louisiana, so Delia sent Isaac to talk sense into her. Isaac wound up kidnapping Fairlee and, in the course of bringing her home to Delia, fell in love with her. Tempest was the youngest of the three—the one with the hottest temper, the darkest blue eyes, and the blackest hair—and she had rubbed him wrong from day one. He sure didn't want to deal with her that morning, when his world had just fallen apart.

She sat down beside him. He didn't need to open his eyes to know that she was wearing those abominable trousers. The first time he'd seen her in them had been the previous year, when he, his brother, Isaac, and cousin, Tyrell, had been sprung from a San Antonio jail to escort Tempest and her sisters back to Louisiana. It was right on the eve of the fall of the Alamo, and Captain Robert Lavalle had offered instant freedom and a nice payment to the three unfairly jailed men to escort three "Sisters" safely to Louisiana. It had seemed the right thing to do at the time, since the women were Catholic nuns and since Bennet's Bluff, Louisiana, was right on their way home to Greenville, Mississippi. For a week on the road the Sisters had halos and wore habits. But when they appeared one morning wearing men's pants, Micah learned right quick that they'd never had halos. It was just a trick of the light.

"Sally died," he said.

"I'm so, so sorry," Tempest said.

"She murdered my father." He blurted it out and wished

immediately he could reach up into the morning breeze and put the words back into his mouth.

Tempest jerked her head around so fast that her neck popped. Her deep blue eyes flashed beneath drawn-down dark eyebrows. Surely she'd misunderstood that statement. A bandit had killed the Burnet brothers' father. He'd shot him in the back for his horse, and they'd caught up with him a day too late in San Antonio, Texas. He'd robbed a bank the day before and gotten himself shot in the process. A bar brawl that night was why Micah, Isaac, and Tyrell had been in the jail and her father had commissioned them to get her and her two sisters out of the area before the fight with Santa Anna began.

"What did you just say?" Tempest asked.

He raked his fingers though his dark brown hair and looked at her through haunted light brown eyes. His strong jaw was angular and his strong chin dimpled in the center. Not enough to be unsightly but enough to give him grief when he shaved.

He had to talk to someone, and he couldn't tell Isaac and Tyrell what he'd just found out. But why did it have to be Tempest who'd decided to go for an early ride that morning?

"What are you doing out alone?" he asked.

"Tell me what you said. Besides, you of all the people in this world would know that I can take care of myself. You rode with me for nearly a month. What would I need an escort for? To aggravate me when I'm already antsy? Now, what was it that you said?" she asked again.

Perhaps if Micah said the words aloud, they would stop burning in his chest. "Give me your absolute promise that you will never tell another soul what I'm about to say."

She cocked her head to one side. "Not even Delia or Fairlee?"

His eyes locked with hers across the foot of space that separated them. "Not anyone. Not even God."

"But He'll hear you when you tell me, and I've got this notion that He already knows anyway," Tempest argued.

"You know what I mean!" Exasperation caused him to rake his fingers through his hair again. If he hadn't already said too much, he'd go home and let the whole sordid tale eat holes in his heart. He'd take it to the grave with him and never tell another soul. He hadn't made a deal with God as Sally had done.

"Okay, okay. Don't get so riled. I won't tell anyone," Tempest agreed.

He took a deep breath and began. "A couple of hours ago the Duval overseer rode over to my house and told me to hurry, that Sally was very sick and calling for me."

"But she was fine on Sunday at the church social," Tempest said.

"She took sick on Monday. She sent a note to tell me to stay away until she was well, but this morning she was calling for me. The doctor said she only had a few hours at the most, and she wanted me by her bedside. Everyone figured it was true love, wanting to hold on until the end. So did I."

"Dear God, do you think all of us who were at the social will come down with her sickness?"

"Let's hope not. When I got there, Sally demanded that everyone else leave the room, even the doctor. They thought that maybe if I was there, she'd rally and get well, but that wasn't why she wanted us to be alone. Once they were out of the room, she told me that she'd killed my father. That she had been sneaking around seeing another man while she was seeing me. My father suspected and caught her at the cabin where they went for their trysts. He was going to tell me, so she shot him and gave his horse to a bank robber on the run from Jackson."

Tempest pinched her arm to prove to herself that she was awake and not dreaming. She'd never liked Sally Duval. The woman's eyes always looked as if they were hiding a big dark secret, but Tempest had never figured on the secret being that huge.

"The eyes never lie," Tempest said.

"What?" Micah asked.

"I said, the eyes don't lie." She laughed, but it never reached her own eyes. "Something about the look in Sally's eyes always bothered me. Now I know what it was. But why did she tell you such a thing? She was going to marry you without telling you, so why now?"

Micah stood up and began to pace. "She said she had promised God that if she could get away with the murder, then she'd confess on her deathbed. She thought she'd outlive me and never have to tell me."

Tempest shivered. "I'm sorry, Micah."

"I'll never trust another woman. Not ever," he said.

She stood too, and held out her hand. "Shake on it."

"You're not going to trust a woman either?" He frowned.

"I decided a long time ago not to trust a man. Not after seeing Matthew Cheval at work courting me back in Louisiana. He was as slimy as a slug."

Micah extended his hand and shook hers. "To not being duped."

Electricity sparked between them. Micah attributed it to her cold hands. Tempest figured it was that his were so warm.

"Now what do you do?" she asked.

"I'm not doing anything. I'm going to forget her and my stupidity."

Tempest shook her head emphatically and put both palms up. "No, you are not. What happened when you left? Tell me what you did after she told you. Talk to me and get it off your chest. And, Micah, you were duped, but you are not stupid."

"I did nothing. I walked out the door, down the stairs, and came directly here."

Tempest planned as she thought. "Your sudden departure could easily be misconstrued as severe shock over losing the love of your life. Now, you are going to send a messenger with a note of condolence to her aunt and uncle. You will attend the funeral. You can be aloof, but you have to be there. Everyone will simply think that you are heartbroken and sick with grief."

"I don't have to do any such thing!" Micah stared at Tempest as if she had two heads and sixteen eyes.

She popped her hands onto her tiny waist and glared at him. "Yes, you will. Not attending will raise questions that you don't want to answer, so you will go, Micah Burnet. Men don't have to cry. They can be all brave and stoic, but you do have to go. Now, you are going home. I'll wait five or ten minutes and follow you. I'll pretend I've just heard the news about Sally's passing and came with condolences from Delia and Tyrell. I'll help you write the note to send over to her relations. You are going to stay in your house all day, and when they bury her, you will be there. You do not have a choice," Tempest said.

"Why?"

"Don't be stupid. If you didn't go to your fiancée's burial, there would be talk. Think about it. Everyone would wonder what she'd said when you were alone that made you refuse to do the right thing." Tempest began to pace. "Tyrell and Isaac would ask questions, and you'd have to tell them."

Micah groaned. "What a mess."

" 'Oh, what a tangled web we weave, when first we practice to deceive,' " she said, quoting an adage that her Aunt Rachel often used.

"Sir Walter Scott said that," Micah said.

"Well, it's the truth whether Scott or Saint Peter came up with it. It's the gospel truth any way you look at it," Tempest said.

"So won't I be deceiving and weaving webs if I pretend I'm a brokenhearted fiancé?" Micah asked.

"Are you?"

He set his jaw in a firm line. "I'm more mad than brokenhearted."

"Then you never loved her, because love conquers all things," Tempest told him, quoting again.

Micah shot her a look that would have fried a lesser woman and the grass surrounding her. "I was going to marry her. She betrayed me. I have a right to be angry."

"Yes, you do. And you would've had the right to break off the engagement if you'd found out about her deception. But now that she's gone and you are the only one who heard the confession, if you don't want anyone to know it, it's in your best interest to pretend. Folks will think you are suffering a broken heart, and in a few months it will all blow over," she said.

He stuck a foot into the stirrup on his horse and slung a leg over the saddle. "You are right, but I don't have to like it."

"Didn't say you had to like it. I'm sure there have been lots of things in your life you didn't like, including me, but you have to get through it. Just like I did," she said.

"What does that mean?" he asked.

"Hey, I didn't like any of you Burnets or Fannins, and I

wound up with two out of the three for brothers-in-law. I'm managing to get through it and even learning to like Isaac and Tyrell, and if I can do that, you can dang sure live through an upset like this."

"Women don't use curse words like that," he said.

She stopped long enough to look up at him. "I never heard Sally use a bad word, saw her ride anything but sidesaddle, or noticed her wearing pants, but she shot your father in the back. Wake up and smell the bacon frying, Micah."

He slapped the reins against the horse's neck and rode off. He hated it when Tempest was right. It hadn't set well with him last year, and it didn't that morning, but it was the truth. And the absolute truth for the future was that he would never trust another woman. The only one he could possibly trust was Tempest, and he'd rather spend his life with Lucifer's sister than a Lavalle woman.

Tempest waited ten minutes before she mounted up and rode toward Micah's house. It was a white two-story house with a deep, shady front porch sporting several massive white pillars. Atop the porch roof was a widow's walk, and another small balcony opened out from the master bedroom. She could imagine Micah's mother and father sitting out there discussing their day when their two sons were young.

She dismounted and looped the reins around a hitching post. She was halfway across the porch when Washington swung the front door open and motioned her inside.

"Mister Micah is in the study. We just heard the bad news about Miss Sally. This will be a sorrowful day in the house. I'm glad you came." He led the way across the wide foyer to an open doorway. "Miss Tempest is here to see you."

"Send her in," Micah said. He faced a blazing fireplace, his back to her. To Tempest's way of thinking, Micah was the best-looking one of the three outlaws who had "rescued" her and her sisters from the Alamo. He was tall and broad-shouldered, and muscles rippled under his snugly fitting shirt. His brown hair was thick and often needed cutting, and his eyes were soft brown.

"Thank you, Washington," Tempest said. "Maybe you could ask Elvira to bring in some tea and food for Micah. I'm sure he hasn't had time for breakfast, and he needs to keep up his strength."

"Yes'm." Washington disappeared toward the kitchen. He wasn't as tall as Micah but didn't miss it by much, and he was just as muscular. He'd been born the same year as Isaac, and the three boys had grown up together on River Bend.

"Now what do we do?" Micah asked.

She removed her coat, hat, and gloves and tossed them onto the settee. "Are you sure, absolutely sure, you don't want to tell Isaac and Tyrell? Or do you want to tell anyone?"

"I do not," he said. "Maybe someday I'll tell Isaac and Tyrell but not right now. They need to pay last respects without that hanging over their heads. The Duvals are our neighbors and friends. They'd be mortified, or else they wouldn't believe me, and that would cause even more problems."

Tempest tucked a few strands of errant hair behind her ears. "Okay, then here's what we do now. Where do I find paper and pen and ink?"

He pointed to the desk. "I cannot make myself write a convincing condolence letter even if you tell me what to say."

"I'll do it," Tempest said.

"Why are you helping me?" Micah asked.

"Because you are kin to my kin, and I wouldn't have either of my sisters or my brothers-in-law—what was it you said?—'mortified' because you did the improper thing. You will stay in this house all day and until the funeral. You can see Ben, your overseer, who will no doubt chalk up everything to a broken heart. And I'm sure Isaac and Tyrell will be here. You'll have to handle those three. I don't think I can do anything about them. We'll rally around you at the graveside, and we'll go to the dinner at the Duvals'."

"I cannot go to that dinner and pretend to be something I'm not. I remember when Mother died what all went on. People coming up to shake my hand and tell me how sorry they were. I can't do that or accept sympathy under these circumstances," he said.

"Leave it to me." She sat down and picked up the pen, dipped it into the inkwell, and began to write. When she finished, she allowed it to dry and read aloud, "Micah Burnet is mourning the loss of his dear fiancée, Sally Duval, and in his indescribable grief he has asked me to convey his heartfelt condolences to her family and to ask that they excuse his absence from the wake. At this point he doesn't feel able to look upon the face of one he loved so much. Sincerely yours, Tempest Lavalle."

"Lord, that sounds so false," he said. "I'm not in mourning for Sally. I'm in shock that she's dead and angry that she killed my father. Are you sure that it's proper for you to write it?"

She nodded. She didn't know if it was proper or not, but it would at least keep Micah from being the talk of the whole western half of Mississippi. Someday the man might get over his anger and fall in love again. If he'd been rude about his fiancée's passing, no decent woman would give him a chance.

"I'm not sure I even loved her, Tempie," he whispered.

Her head shot up so fast that it made her dizzy. Only her

sisters called her Tempie, but she and Micah now shared a secret. Did that gave him liberty to call her by her nickname?

"Sure, you did. If you hadn't loved her, you never would have proposed to her. When you have eaten something, you are going up to your room. Stay there all day. As of this minute, you are consumed with grief and can't see anyone," Tempest said.

"I'll go mad with boredom," he grumbled.

"Then send Washington for me sometime in the afternoon. As kin of kin, it wouldn't be improper for me to sit with you, perhaps read to you to help relieve the headache brought on by grief," she said.

" 'Grief'? More like pent-up pure old mad," he said.

"Get over it, Micah," Tempest said seriously.

"How?"

"Don't dwell on it."

His soft brown eyes went hard. "That's easier said than done."

She met his gaze and didn't flinch. "I didn't say it was easy. It might be the hardest thing you ever have to do. Even harder than losing your father. But you can do it. You have strength and character. You come from good stock."

Elvira brought in a tray with a basket of warm biscuits, coffee, butter, and strawberry jam. She was as round as she was tall, wore her graying kinky hair cut close to her scalp, and her dark eyes missed nothing. She'd been with the Burnet family since before Isaac was born. As the best healer and midwife on River Bend, she had brought Isaac and Micah, as well as Washington and her newest kitchen help, Cherish, into the world. Her calico dress was starched and ironed, but her white bibbed apron had a few stains on the front where it had caught flecks of the boiling soup she'd been stirring.

"Will you be pouring the coffee for him, Miss Tempest?" she asked.

"Yes, and as soon as I get him to eat a few bites, he will be retiring to his room for the rest of the day. He's just come from the Duval house, where Sally passed this morning," Tempest said.

"Washington told me. I'm sorry. That's a hard thing to bear."

Tempest followed Elvira to the door and shut it firmly. When she turned around, Micah was already on his second biscuit and had poured coffee for both of them.

"Usually grief doesn't want to eat like a horse," she said bluntly.

"But anger does," he shot right back at her. "If you want some of this, you'd best get after it."

Tempest groaned. "You know what the servants will say? That you couldn't have eaten that whole platter of food when your heart was broken. They'll be spreading it around that I ate it. And right after hearing that Sally has passed. I've just become the most unladylike woman in all of Mississippi."

He picked up another biscuit and slathered butter on it. "Sounds good to me. It can be payback for all the horrible things you put me through on the trip from San Antonio."

She grabbed a biscuit and stuffed two teaspoons of jam inside it. Their hands brushed, and the sparks flew again. "Me! You were the horrid one. Always acting so superior because women weren't supposed to wear britches or carry guns."

"Come to think of it, you *are* unladylike, Tempie Lavalle." It was their fighting that caused his hand to tingle. A good, rousting fight that was doing wonders to erase the heaviness from his heart.

"At least I'm honest."

"You are definitely that. Now, I'm taking my account books up to my room. I'll work on them until you see fit to come back to 'console' me this afternoon. What a mess this is, Tempie." He had proposed to a woman but hadn't loved her the way Isaac did Fairlee or the way Tyrell did Delia. He'd hoped that time would produce the kind of love that his brother and cousin shared with their wives. That someday Sally would learn to love him as deeply as Delia and Fairlee loved their husbands. Maybe fate had saved him after all. Hopefully he would find answers to all the questions plaguing him when the dust settled.

"Yes, it is a mess," Tempest replied. "I'll send Washington with your note and one from Delia and Fairlee. By the time I return, I should have information about the burial."

He picked up two large binders and started toward the door. "Thank you."

"Bet it hurt like the very devil to say that, didn't it?" she said.

"You will never know how much."

Chapter Two

"Delia, where are you?" Tempest yelled from the foyer.

Delia's voice carried out of the room to Tempest's left. "In the parlor with the baby. Where have you been?"

She tossed her hat and coat onto a chair beside the credenza and rushed into the room. "Bad news. Sally died this morning."

Delia's crystal-clear blue eyes filled with tears. "Poor Micah. Tyrell and I must go to him immediately. We'll send a note over to the Duvals. They'll be devastated along with Micah. How did you find out?"

"Micah was returning from there, and I met him while I was out riding. Our paths crossed, and he told me. I followed him home and wrote a note for him, which I'm going to have Washington take over to the Duvals' place with one from us. He can bring back news of when the burial will be, and we'll make plans to attend. Sally asked for Micah to come to her in her dying moments," Tempest said.

"How is he holding up? This is just horrible. She was such a sweet woman."

Tempest bit her tongue and thought: *Sweet enough to kill Micah's father to cover up a tryst with her true love. Sweet enough to marry him and not confess. That's not* sweet, *dear sister, but I can't say a word about it. I didn't realize how difficult this was going to be. My sisters and I have always shared everything, but I've given my word not to tell a soul about this.*

"Well?" Delia asked.

"I'm sorry. I was thinking of all we need to do. Micah's grieving. I'll go back this afternoon and see if there's anything I can do for him. He said he's not up to talking to anyone right now, but he might like some company later to help him get through the long hours of the day." Tempest sat down on the settee and reached for Etta Ruth.

Delia handed the baby over and began to pace the floor. "That's a generous offer from you, knowing how you feel about Micah. Maybe you could ride on over to Fairlee and Isaac's place and let them know, so they can be prepared for the funeral. I'm sure they'll put her in the church cemetery."

Tempest nodded. That was another reason never to tell what had happened, because the church would frown on burying a murderer in its cemetery. As if a dead person could keep another from entering the Pearly Gates merely by being buried next to him or her.

"Do you suppose they'll bury her tomorrow?" Tempest asked.

"Not that soon. Maybe the day after." Delia went to a small desk and began to write a note to her neighbors. "How is Micah doing?"

"Men don't show their emotions like we women do," Tempest said.

"What happened to Sally? Do you have any details?" Delia asked, as she dipped the pen and wrote.

"Just that she came down sick after the church social on Sunday. I'm so glad you stayed home with Etta Ruth. Whatever Sally caught, it must have gotten into her lungs, because this morning the doctor said he couldn't do anything else for her and that she only had a few hours to live. She died before Micah left." Tempest reminded herself to keep it simple and tell the whole story, only leaving out the most important detail.

"In his arms? Oh, the agony of it," Delia said.

"Man don't know how the good Lord done looked down on him today." Mama Glory brought in a tray with tea and cookies. "We done got word that Sally has passed on and that Mister Micah was there. I never did like that girl. She wasn't the one for Mister Micah. That one was out to get a rich husband."

"Mama Glory!" Delia gasped.

Mama Glory had closely cropped graying hair and a round face full of wrinkles and age. She and Elvira had been with the family since before Micah and Isaac were born and had helped raise all three boys, depending on whether they were at Morris and Franny Burnet's house or at Luke and Amelia Fannin's. The two women were sisters, and they shared River Bend, the plantation.

Mama Glory had lived long enough and gained enough trust and authority that she spoke her mind and didn't care who was boss. She might be listed on the books as the property of the Burnet-Fannin plantation, but that didn't mean a blessed thing to her.

"I agree with Mama Glory. I thought she was marrying

Micah because of his money instead of love," Tempest said honestly.

"Tempie! Momma said we should never speak ill of the dead," Delia said.

"Well, it's the truth, though I won't stand up at the graveside tomorrow and say it aloud. I'm just saying it to my sister and to Mama Glory," Tempest said.

Mama Glory mumbled as she poured the tea. "Woman ought not to look at other men, including Mister Isaac and Mister Tyrell, if she's in love with Mister Micah. Woman what demands a fancy ring from a man to show the world that she's been asked for ain't got the right thing on her mind. If she was in love, then her heart would show the world she'd been asked for and was about to promise the good Lord that she'd be his wife until she died. I heard she asked for Mister Micah at the end. Wonder what she said to him."

Delia shook her head and went back to writing. "Aunt Rachel always said that the walls have ears, but I don't suppose they'll be talking. I'm sure Sally wanted Micah to know that she was taking his love with her to eternity and would be waiting for him."

Tempest kept her head down. If Sally was waiting on Micah in the next life, there was going to be a fight so big, it might blow the Pearly Gates right off their hinges. "Momma said to be careful what you say because the walls might repeat what they heard, and it would be carried on the wind to the next room, the next plantation, and all over the entire state," she said pointedly, for Mama Glory's benefit.

"You ain't got nothin' to be worryin' about me sayin' a word. I'm not glad she's dead. I'm just glad Mister Micah ain't goin' to marry her. I wish she and that cousin of hers would have stayed off down in another part of the world. I never did like either one of them." Mama Glory muttered all the way out the door.

"Are you sure it's proper for you to be traipsing over to Micah's?" Delia asked.

"It's a well-known fact that I'm certainly not fond of Micah. Besides, lightning might strike in the same place twice, but it would take a miracle for it to strike three times in the same place. I'm safe, dear sister. You and Fairlee paid the price."

Delia smiled. "I'm thinking that Tyrell and Isaac paid the price. Fairlee and I are reaping the benefits."

"Well, that's a nice way to look at it, and I'm glad you do, but the results are still the same. If I was ever inclined to trust a man with my heart, that man would not be Micah Burnet. And after this morning, I doubt he'll ever trust a woman again," Tempest said.

"Why wouldn't he trust a woman? Sally didn't *plan* to accept his proposal and then die before the wedding. His heart will heal, and he'll find someone who will make him happy," Delia said.

Tempest bit her lip. She'd already said too much. "I'm going to ride over to Isaac and Fairlee's now and then come back by Micah's place. Washington will pick up your note on his way to the Duvals'. Anything you want to send with me for Fairlee?"

Delia signed the short letter and stood up. "Yes, I've got some threads she'll need soon for the pillowcases she's embroidering. Play with the baby while I fetch them. Will you be home in time for dinner?"

"No, but I will be here for supper," Tempest said.

She waited until her sister had left the room before she

held Etta Ruth up and looked right into her blue eyes. "Your papa thinks the sun comes up each day just to shine on your pretty face. But don't ever use your beauty like Sally did. It won't be worth it in the end. Grow up to be as independent as your momma, darlin'."

"I hope she does, and I do think that the sun is there for her beckoning, as well as the moon and stars. Now, what was it that Sally used her beauty for? I never thought she was all that pretty. Nice enough and seemed to dote on Micah, but not beautiful like Delia." Tyrell leaned on the doorjamb. It was easy to picture him as Micah and Isaac's cousin. Tyrell's face was only a little rounder, and his brown eyes were a darker shade and his mouth a little fuller.

"When did you come in?" Tempest avoided the question. She'd have to be careful what she said, even to her infant niece. The walls *did* have ears.

Tyrell crossed the room and held out his arms for his daughter. "Just walked in the door and kissed my beautiful wife as she went up to get some thread for Fairlee. She told me the sad news. I'll go on over to see Micah right away. I understand Washington is taking our condolences to the Duval family. I'll ride over there this afternoon to see if there's anything else we can help with. Delia said that you'd seen Micah. How's he taking it?"

Tempest's mind flapped around in circles searching for a single reason Tyrell and Isaac shouldn't go to see Micah. She finally resolved that she'd done what she could to shield him from well-wishers. He'd have to deal with his brother and cousin.

"Tempest?" Tyrell asked.

"I'm sorry. I was thinking of all that we'll need to get ready before the funeral. I suppose it will be in a couple of days.

Micah is actually taking it very well, but you know what a private person he is. He didn't want to see anyone, so he's spending the time inside. I wrote his condolence note for him." She stumbled over the words as if they were sharp rocks in her path.

"I'm sure he appreciates that, and I understand how he must feel. If it were Delia, I'm afraid I'd turn into a hermit and depend on my memories to keep me alive. It's going to be a rough time ahead for Micah," Tyrell said seriously.

"Did you like Sally?" Tempest asked.

Tyrell hesitated as if he had to think before he spoke. "She wasn't Delia. I don't expect many people get blessed with what Delia and I have together. But she would have been a good wife to Micah, I'm sure. She seemed to be very fond of him."

Tempest read between the lines. Tyrell hadn't answered her with a yes or no. He wasn't speaking ill of the dead, but he wasn't going to tell a lie, either. That was the second time she'd heard that word, *fond,* that morning. When Micah was telling her the details of Sally's death, he'd mentioned that she'd said she was *fond* of him. Wasn't a person supposed to be in *love* when she married, not just in *fond?*

"Yes, she was," Tempest said. "I hear Delia. I'll be leaving to take the news to Fairlee. You want me to tell Isaac anything?"

"Tell him we'll meet at Micah's in an hour," Tyrell said.

Tempest nodded. She took the threads from Delia and shoved them deep inside her pocket. "See you at suppertime. Please ask Dotty to get our black dresses ready for the funeral. We don't have to wear black for a full year, do we? They weren't married yet. And we didn't even wear black for a year when Momma and Daddy both passed."

"No, but we'll have to forego any spring parties or socials. You won't be meeting any eligible bachelors until fall," Delia said.

"And that is the silver lining," Tempest said, as she marched across the floor and out the door.

Washington ushered Tempest into the house for the second time that day. He led the way to the library and knocked on the door. "Mister Micah, Miss Tempest is here to see you again."

"Send her in," Micah said in a strong voice.

"Yes, sir." Washington opened the double doors wide and stood to one side. When she was inside, he left the doors open and went back to cleaning the silver in the kitchen for Elvira.

"Shall I shut the doors?" Tempest asked.

"Only if you want to suffer the backlash of talk saying that you are already trying to take Sally's place," he said bluntly.

"Dear God, open up all the doors in the whole house and the windows too," she snapped.

A smile turned the corners of his mouth up. "The feeling is mutual, I assure you."

Tempest sat down in the rocking chair close to the window looking out over the front yard. "I thought you were going to stay in your room and be the grief-stricken fiancé."

"I changed my mind. There's not a desk up there big enough for my ledgers, and I'm not going to be driven to my room when I can work here. If anyone other than family arrives, Washington is to show them to the parlor, where you are going to relay my heartfelt thanks and tell them that I'm not seeing people today. They won't know if I'm in here or lying on my bed soaking my pillows with tears, will they?"

"That's pretty harsh," she said.

"Not as harsh as talk is going to be when people arrive to find you dressed like that after the death of an almost-relative." His eyes went from the tips of her boots, up her britches, over the hat in her lap to her hair, which was a fright from wearing said hat and riding in the wind. Curly strands had found their way from the braids wrapped around her head and were dangling down her back.

"Dang! I wasn't expecting to play hostess," she said.

"That foul language goes with your britches very well, my lady," he said.

Tempest clenched her hands into fists. "I'm not your lady."

"And that is the first good news I've had today."

"If you are going to be hateful, I'm going home," she said.

Micah threw up both hands defensively. "Stay. I really don't expect that anyone will come by, since they'll all gather at the Duvals' place. I'm hoping your note will keep them away at least until the funeral, which, by the way, is going to be at four o'clock tomorrow evening in the church. Burial will follow and a supper at the Duval house. We will attend all of it."

"We, as in the whole family?" Tempest asked.

"That's right. It's easier than telling Isaac and Tyrell why I don't want to be there. I can do this, Tempie," Micah said.

His rush of anger had subsided and been replaced with numbness. There would be no wedding in the early summer, no children to run and play in his house. No little Etta Ruth look-alike to grow up and stamp her feet when she couldn't have a pony before she was old enough. No wife to keep his bed warm at night.

"Of course you can. Was not telling Isaac and Tyrell difficult?" she asked.

"It was tougher than telling you 'thank you' earlier," he said.

"Then you are a strong man, Micah. And with that kind of strength you will get through these next days. Delia says we can't have spring parties or go to any but that we don't have to wear black for a year, since Sally wasn't officially family."

"Well, we must do what Delia says," he said coldly.

Tempest came out of the chair so fast that she was barely a blur in his peripheral vision. "Don't you be snide about my sister. She's only trying to do the right thing."

"I wasn't," Micah said defensively. "I was actually thinking that I need to thank you again for getting me out of such things. I really don't like those spring parties that we always have to attend to keep up appearances. They aren't anything but glorified mating rituals."

Tempest blushed. "Is that any way to talk to a lady?"

"Probably not. But then, I wasn't talking to a lady. I was talking to you, Tempie, and you are no lady."

She crossed her arms over her chest and glared at him. "That would be the pot calling the kettle black, wouldn't it?"

For the first time since daybreak, when Sally confessed her sin and then drew her last breath, Micah felt human again. "Does that mean you think I'm not a gentleman?"

She locked gazes with him and refused to back down. "I'd say we're a matched pair. I speak my mind, and you do the same. If I'd been born a man or if you'd been born a woman, we could have been very good friends."

He put his accounting to the side and leaned back in his chair. "Want a cigar?"

"Good God, Micah, I do not smoke!"

He smiled again. "Drink?"

"Women in my family only drink when they get the vapors, which is never."

"Guess we wouldn't have been such good friends, then, would we? I would have thought you quite the pious sissy if you refused a good cigar and a shot of aged whiskey or after-dinner brandy," he said.

Tempest shrugged. "I guess we wouldn't have. Now, what can I do to help this afternoon? I'll go crazy just sitting in a chair and watching the grass grow."

"Are you any good at untangling a mess in my accounting books? I've got a problem that I can't find. One side won't balance with the other," he said.

She stood up and stretched, raising her hands high over her head and bending from one side to the other.

Micah had never seen a woman do that before. Men, yes, when they were out on a long trail ride or even out in the field, when the afternoon sun beat down upon their heads, but not a woman. The way the sun's rays flowed in the window, highlighting those heavy ropes of curly black hair twisted around her head, it appeared that she did have a shiny halo listing a bit to the left and floating a couple of inches from the top of her head. But Tempie wouldn't fool Micah again. That was nothing but a trick of the light to cover up her horns.

She crossed the room in a dozen easy strides and looked over his shoulder. "I'm very good at long lines of figures. Uncle Jonathan and I often spent hours in the study getting his books to balance. Show me the problem, and we'll find the mistake."

"Drag up a chair. Don't peer over my shoulder," he said.

Her warm breath on his neck sent shivers down his spine. Sally had never affected him like that, but then, she'd never been that close to him. She'd hugged him very briefly the night that he proposed and allowed him to brush a brief kiss across her lips. Even that hadn't caused a quick intake of his breath or his heart to pitch in an extra beat. It had to be the crazy day still manifesting itself in more emotional upheaval, he decided.

"Don't be bossy with me," she smarted off. She brought a straight-backed chair from the corner and set it right next to him. "Okay, show me the accounts, and give me some paper to figure on."

He handed her an extra pen, nodded toward the inkwell, which she'd already used that morning, and pointed at the clean paper on a corner of the desk. "I've figured it six times and can't find my mistake, but I'm off by several hundred dollars."

She ran a finger down each side of the ledger. "Seems strange to be doing this today, doesn't it? It's as if you and Sally were never . . ."

He nodded. "The anger is passing. My father said that life works out the way it should. What Sally did surely would have caused problems between us after a while. I don't wish her gone at such a young age, but . . ."

Her finger stopped. "I understand. It's hard to put into words, isn't it? Here's the first mistake. You added the price of five bolts of calico for the servants' dresses instead of subtracting it."

He picked up his pen and scratched through the numbers, subtracting rather than adding. "That takes care of a portion of it. Let's see if we can find the rest of it."

"Whoa!" Tempest exclaimed.

He jumped back as if he'd touched a hot poker with his bare fingers. "What did I do?"

She pointed to the ledger. "It wasn't anything you did right then. It's what you did last week. You subtracted here rather than added, and it's within a dollar of the same amount of what you added before, so we are back to the beginning."

He moaned. "I swear I'd give the books to Tyrell or Isaac if they'd have them, but they say they'd do a worse job than I do."

"Why don't you get me some clean ledger pages and let me start all over on this year's business? You've got so many strike-through numbers that it's hard to figure."

He opened a drawer and removed a dozen fresh pages, then removed the old pages and laid them aside. "Mother used to keep the accounts for the plantation. My father never was good with numbers, but he could make cotton and tobacco grow out of rocks."

Tempest numbered the clean sheets and bent her head to the work. Working with figures and keeping books was something that she enjoyed. "Okay, first mistake right here, back on the first day of the new year."

In a nervous gesture, Micah raked his fingers through his hair and watched her enter numbers as neatly as his mother had done. "Don't suppose I could hire you to take care of this for the plantation, could I?"

She nodded. "I'll do it for free. How about every Friday afternoon? I'll come over right after lunch and do the entering and balancing. If I do it every week, it shouldn't get tangled up like this again."

Micah's eyes widened. "Are you serious?"

She looked up into his dark brown eyes and nodded. "If I'm going to live on this plantation, I might as well make myself useful for something other than running embroidery thread back and forth between my two older sisters."

Chapter Three

In a bold move, Constance Duval took Micah's hands in hers and pulled him down beside her on the settee in the parlor of the Duval home. "My dear Micah, Sally loved you more than life itself, and she was more like a sister than a cousin to me. Aunt Edith gave me her ring as a keepsake. I'm hoping that is all right with you."

"You are welcome to have it," Micah said. He didn't want the ring to remind him that Sally was only marrying him because he was the better catch. Every time he looked at it, he'd think about Frank, who'd left five minutes before she did that fatal day.

"I'll always wear it on a chain around my neck. It wouldn't be proper to put it on my finger, since it was a token of your undying and eternal love for her."

The ruby and gold ring that he'd ordered from New York City dangled on a long black velvet ribbon around Constance's neck. She placed a hand on it, and smiled up at Micah through the tears flowing down her round face and dripping onto her black mourning dress.

Micah attempted to pull his hands away, but she held on tightly. "I'll need you to comfort me when the memories are too much to handle. I'm glad we are neighbors and I can call on you anytime I wish."

Tempest was standing in a corner, but she didn't miss a single word of Constance's laying a foundation to be the next Mrs. Burnet. What an absolute crock of balderdash! A strumpet off the streets wouldn't go after a grieving man on the very day his fiancée was buried. Poor Micah looked like a rabbit caught in a trap with a dozen snapping, hungry wolves circling around to see which could get to him first.

Constance had a washtub full of gall to flutter her eyelashes at Micah before her cousin was cold in the grave. Tempest could easily see her as the lead wolf, with her claws sharpened and her fangs bared against all the other wolves. The poor little cottontail named Micah was vulnerable, and she intended to make the first move.

Micah's eyes widened when he caught Tempest's gaze. She nodded slightly and set her coffee cup down on a table before strolling over in that direction to chase away the big old mean wolf and spring the trap to rescue him.

"Hello, Constance. I'm so very sorry for your loss. I know you will miss Sally and it will be a very hard year for you. Will you be going back to Jackson anytime soon?" Tempest said.

Constance gave her an icy glare. "Of course not. I'm needed here to comfort Aunt Edith and Uncle Vincent. They, of course, are heartbroken. They never had a daughter of their own and adored both Sally and me."

"I'm sure you will be a great help to them through it all." Tempest smiled.

Micah pulled his hand free from Constance and fairly

jumped to his feet. "Are you and the rest of the family ready to go now?" he asked Tempest.

Tempest shook her head. "Fairlee and Delia are with dear Edith. But I do have a horrid headache coming on. Perhaps Washington wouldn't mind making two trips. He could take me home and come back for the rest of our family."

"I'll go with you. You shouldn't go alone with a headache. You might need someone with you," Micah said.

"You'll be going right past the cemetery," Constance said. "Maybe I'll go along and see the grave, now that it's all filled in. I could spend a while there, and when you come back for the rest of the family, you could pick me up." Constance let a fresh batch of tears loose to stream down her cheeks.

Tempest threw an arm around Constance's shoulders. "Darlin', it's too soon for you. Wait a week. Time will heal your broken heart and make it so much easier to look upon the final resting place by then."

Constance's eyes flashed enough heat and anger that, if looks could have killed, Tempest Lavalle would have been nothing but a pile of bones on Edith Duval's fine imported carpet. "Of course, you are right. Will Micah be all right?"

"I'm sure he will. The Burnet men are very strong," Tempest said. Then she leaned over and whispered softly, "But he does need time to heal before you strangle him to death with that ribbon and ring around your neck."

Constance turned quickly and buried her face in Tempest's shoulder, whispering back, "You witch. You just want him for yourself."

Tempest patted her back. "Darlin', you can have him and the ring. I don't want him. Never did and never will."

"Liar!" Constance said.

"Be careful. The last woman who called me a liar suffered

two black eyes and a bald spot on the back of her head," Tempest whispered.

Constance took two steps back and smiled brightly through another river of fake tears. "Do let me know if I can be of any help to the Burnet or Fannin families."

Tempest smiled back. "Thank you. If we need you, we'll send Washington or Benjamin over promptly with a summons."

Micah said good-bye to both Edith and Vincent Duval and ushered Tempest out of the house. Washington was dozing with his chin on his chest when Micah touched his leg.

"Yes, sir." Washington picked up the reins. "Will the rest of the family be along?"

"Not right now. You'll be taking me and Miss Tempie to Tyrell's and coming back for them." Micah opened the door for Tempest and helped her inside the coach.

"I thought she was going to loop that velvet ribbon around your neck and drag you back to the church with it," Tempest said, giggling, once they were seated and the coach was in motion.

Micah rolled his brown eyes toward the ceiling of the carriage. "Why did she act like that?"

"A man is never more vulnerable than he is right after the death of a loved one. A woman on the prowl for a husband can swoop right in and set up a foundation for building a new name right there. It'll be improper for Constance to go to parties or dance this spring, and she must wear black, but it would be very understandable for her to console her cousin's heartsick fiancé."

"Sounds like balderdash to me," Micah grumbled.

"It is."

"Why didn't you warn me that she might do that?"

Tempest opened the side curtain to let the sunlight inside. It was a lovely spring day, more conducive to a picnic than a funeral. "I didn't think about it, or I would have."

"Really? Or were you standing over there laughing at me all the while?" Micah asked.

Tempest pointed out the window. "There's a deer and twin fawns. Hurry, you'll miss them."

He leaned forward and looked out the window. "You didn't answer me."

Tempest slapped him on the arm. "I was not laughing. I heard every word, but I was waiting for a sign from you to rescue you. For all I knew, you were enjoying every minute of the charade and thinking about taking that ring from the ribbon and putting it on her finger. Poor Edith and Vincent have no idea what their nieces are like, do they?"

Micah shook his head. "I don't suppose they do. Edith and Vincent were friends of both my parents and Tyrell's all these years. They'd be devastated to know what has happened."

"Or what Constance has in mind?" Tempest asked.

"What did she say to you when you two were hugging each other?"

"A catfight, darlin', is between two women. They do not share the details with the tomcats. Suffice it to say that she knows I'm on to her, and that might give you a little bit of breathin' room."

Micah cocked his head to one side. "Did you just call me darlin'?"

"Of course I did. I call Tyrell and Isaac that on occasion too. Especially when I'm being sarcastic. Don't get all worked up over it. I don't have you or your farmhouse in my sights for the future."

"Thank God. I've had all the women I can stand for a few years," Micah growled, and he leaned back in the seat.

"Darlin'—and that's meant sarcastically again, so don't jump out of the carriage and head for the hills—you'd better get ready to send a dozen notes of regret a week over to the Duval house if you've had all the women you can stand," Tempest said.

"Why's that?"

"Constance is going to invent reasons to invite you to dinner. Or maybe she'll need you to come desperately to console her when she finds a hairpin on the floor that belonged to Sally. Then there will be the long walks," Tempest said.

"Walks?" Micah frowned.

"Oh, yes. Only long strolls along the river or sitting in Edith's flower garden with you beside her will keep her from crying that morning or afternoon or evening."

Micah raked his fingers through his hair, a gesture that Tempest had already attributed to nervousness or frustration. "What am I to do?"

"Don't ever start going over there. Make excuses from day one. Be gentle so that Edith and Vincent don't think you are an uncaring rat, but keep in mind that right now you are Constance's pot of gold at the end of the rainbow. We are nearly to Tyrell's. Want to saddle up a couple of horses and go for a ride?"

"Sun is setting. It's too late. Besides, I thought you had a headache," he said.

Tempest sighed. "I suppose it is too late. But I left my headache back there at the Duvals'. Its name is Constance."

Washington brought the carriage to a halt in front of the house. "We're here, Mister Micah."

"I may never leave this plantation again," Micah sighed

as he crawled out of the carriage. Tempest Lavalle was the only woman he'd ever known who looked stunning in black funeral dress. Her flawless complexion was even creamier against the black silk dress buttoned up to her neck. The small velvet hat with a short veil over her face was almost seductive. When he put his hands on her slim waist to set her from the door of the carriage to the ground, his heart did another of those flips that confused him.

"Find a hole and dive into it until Constance gets tired of trying to find a way to get you to the altar. Oh, I forgot the old 'make an honest woman of me' ploy." Tempest led the way onto the porch.

"Washington, I'm sure the others will be ready by the time you get back. If not, go around to the back door and tell the cook that you haven't had supper," Micah said before he followed her inside.

"Now tell me. What is this honest-woman thing?" Micah asked when they were in the parlor.

Mama Glory rushed into the room before Tempest could answer. "Miss Tempest, how many of you are going to be here for supper? You'll be stayin', Mister Micah. I've got a ham, and I know how you like my ham. Did any of the people from over at the Duval place come home with you?"

"No. We snuck out. Constance was trying to get a hook into Micah," Tempest tattled.

"Oh, lawsy! You can't be lettin' that happen, Mister Micah. God only takes care of fools one time. You get yourself all tangled up in hot water again, and He'll just let you stew in it. That woman is worse than her cousin. Person oughtn't to be speakin' ill of the dead, or else their ghosts will come and haunt them at night, so I can't be sayin' much more. Old woman like me would drop down dead as a chicken with its head done cut off if she took to seein' ghosties in the night. Scary thing it is, talkin' ill of the dead. But you got to watch yourself. Your mother made me promise her on her deathbed that I'd see to it you boys was all took care of, and you're the last of the brood," Mama Glory fussed.

Tempest waited until Mama Glory sucked up another big chestful of air and said, "We could use a pot of tea and some of those cookies you made yesterday."

"Yes'm, I can do that, but, Miss Tempest, you got to promise me that you won't be lettin' that Duval woman get her hands on Mister Micah. She ain't the woman for him. I feel it in my old bones," Mama Glory said.

"I'll make her so mad that she won't want to come into this house, but he's going to have to make up excuses to stay off her place," Tempest said. There was no need for her to be taking *all* the responsibility for a man who raised her own ire to the boiling level nearly every time she was in the same room with him.

"Yes'm, he is, and he will." Mama Glory gave Micah a knowing look and shook her finger at him as she left the room.

"I never expected to be having a conversation like this during the time of a funeral," Micah said.

"Me, either. At Mother's funeral we were all so sad and somber, I thought the sky would fall in on top of us."

"Us too. And we were so busy trying to catch my father's murderer that we didn't have time to grieve for long. You were going to tell me about the honest-woman thing."

Tempest sank into a comfortable chair. No sitting on the edge of it the way Constance had in the Duval parlor. Tempie didn't have to be a lady in her sister's house or in front of Micah. "Sit down and make yourself at home. The honest-woman thing goes like this. If all else fails and she's determined to have you, then she will connive to get you alone for an entire night. Maybe the carriage you are riding in throws a wheel, and you are forced to spend the night with her in a barn. Or she might simply crawl into bed with you late some night, and you'll awake to her beside you and weeping about how you seduced her. There's no end to the possibilities. Many a man has been brought to his knees because he wanted to do the right thing."

"That's no way for a lady to be talking. And how do you know all these things?" Micah asked.

"A dress does not make a lady any more than a habit makes a nun. Suffice it to say that I've seen the honest-woman thing happen before," Tempest answered.

"Women are evil," he muttered.

"We aren't born with golden halos or big fluffy white wings," Tempest agreed, laughing.

"Amen to that," Micah said.

Chapter Four

Tempest stuck a foot into the stirrup and threw a leg up over the saddle. This would be her second Friday to ride over to Micah's to do book work. The previous week she hadn't even seen him. Hopefully, today would be the same. Sharing a secret of such huge magnitude made her plumb nervous, and every time they were alone, that was the first topic that came up.

Since the funeral he'd come to dinner at Tyrell and Delia's three times. Mama Glory had fussed over him and made his favorite meals. Delia had patted his arm and asked how he was doing. Tyrell had engaged him in conversation about the new crops going into the ground. Everyone except Tempest treated him like a mourning, lovesick fiancé.

She rode out of the stables and took a deep breath. Spring had finally pushed winter completely out of the picture, and the afternoon air was perfect. Not too hot to make her work up a sweat on her ride from one corner of the plantation to the middle of it. Not a bit of nip in the air to require a jacket.

Fairlee had ridden over that morning, and the three sisters

had spent the whole forenoon out in the flower garden. It had been let go to seed for years, and Delia was determined that she'd have a place worthy of a garden party by the time Etta was big enough to celebrate her birthday with little friends invited. Fairlee had sketched a design for the shrubs and roses, the pathways and the flower beds. It wasn't so elaborate as to be impossible, but it would be a big undertaking. Tyrell had promised that he'd take two or three men from the fields to do her bidding, and Mama Glory had smiled all morning.

"Yes'm, it's going to be a beautiful thing to have Mister Tyrell's momma's gardens back. You are doing a good thing," she'd said.

The idea of Etta Ruth growing up with ribbons in her dark hair and having a party put a smile onto Tempest's face. But it faded quickly when she was greeted at the door by a long-faced Washington. He usually smiled when she arrived and showed her directly to the office, where she set about putting all of Micah's notes and scribbles onto one sheet of paper and then transposing them to the ledger. It was work that she enjoyed as much as helping design flower gardens.

"Mister Micah is out with his brother, and Miss Constance Duval is in the parlor," he said.

If moods could be described in colors, Tempest's went from a cheery yellow to menacing black in a split second. "I see. Well, I suppose I should stop by there first. Is he coming home anytime soon?"

Washington shook his head. "I don't think so, and she says she's staying until he does. Should I tell Elvira to bring tea or coffee?"

Tempest removed her riding gloves and stuck them into the back pocket of her trousers. "Yes, and something to eat."

Constance sat on the edge of a chair with her back so straight that she looked horribly uncomfortable. When Tempest opened the door, she was holding the ring around her neck and smiling brightly. The moment she saw that it wasn't Micah, the sweet expression turned into a frown, and she let go of the ring. Tempest watched it fall to the end of the velvet ribbon.

Constance snarled her nose and narrowed her eyes as her gaze started at Tempest's boot tips and traveled up her pants legs to her button-down cotton shirt tucked in and cinched with a wide black leather belt. Her nostrils flared in disgust as she glared at Tempest's hair in disarray where the wind had whipped sections from the chaste bun at the nape of her neck.

"Hello, Constance." Tempest crossed the room and sat down on a settee, sinking back into the soft, comfortable cushions and stretching her legs out in front of her.

"You look horrible," Constance said.

"Well, you look positively radiant. Black becomes you, and that style is good on you. You should have more dresses made from that pattern when you get to shed the mourning clothing. It positively enhances your figure." Tempest removed her hat and laid it on a side table. "Washington tells me that Micah is out with Isaac. I've sent orders by him to Elvira to bring us some refreshments. I expect you'd like a cup of tea or coffee and maybe a cookie or two?"

Constance pointed a long, slim finger at her. "You are not the lady of this house, Tempest Lavalle."

"No, thank goodness, I am not. But I am a relative of sorts, and it would be a shame for you to have come all this way for naught and not even have a cup of tea."

"What is it that you do here?" Constance asked.

"Just a little bit of secretarial work. Now tell me, how is everyone doing over at the Duval place? Is Edith any better? I've been meaning to get over there to visit with her, but I've been so busy. You know that Isaac and Fairlee are building a house, and Delia has Etta Ruth, and we all dote on her. Then Delia decided to bring back the flower garden to its original beauty. It'll take more than one year, but we're designing and working on that in addition to trying to run a plantation." Tempest deliberately went on and on to keep Constance from asking any more questions about her job.

Constance wiped her eyes with the tip of one forefinger. "Poor Sally would have been their sister-in-law and been a part of all that. I should go and see each of them. I'm sure there is still an ache in their hearts at losing her. She would have fit in so well here on River Bend. And how is our dear Micah? Is he holding up well or still grieving like he was at the funeral? I've never seen a man in so much pain."

Tempest wondered if they were talking about the same man. Micah had seemed aloof and bewildered at the funeral but not in pain. "Micah is doing very well. He's been to dinner a few times at Delia's, and he appears to be losing himself in his work. With the planting season on us, there's never enough daylight to get everything done, is there?"

Constance placed a hand over her heart in a dramatic gesture. "Oh, my, no!"

Cherish brought in a tray with coffee and tea. Elvira came in behind her, carrying a plate with cookies and tiny slices of cinnamon-raisin bread. "Anything else, Miss Tempie?" Elvira asked.

"Thank you but no. This will be just fine. Just set it right here, and I'll pour," Tempest answered.

The look on Constance's face left no doubt that she did not like the servants looking to Tempest as if she were the lady of the house. No doubt Constance was making herself a solemn vow that she would be pouring tea and coffee here before the year was out, and Tempest would not be welcome in her home. She'd probably put Elvira, Cherish, and even Washington out of the house and train her own servants to listen only to her. Constance would not want to be outdone by a woman who wore britches and slumped in a settee like a hoyden.

Tempest sat up and picked up a cookie. "Now, where were we? Oh, yes, about the rose bushes. Coffee or tea?"

"Coffee is fine," Constance said icily.

Tempest poured them each a cup and handed Constance's to her. She was sorely tempted to accidentally drop it into her lap, but then Constance would have to stay until her dress could be cleaned and dried, and Tempest might strangle her in that length of time. There had never been a woman who'd gotten under Tempest's skin like Constance Duval. Sally had been engaged to Micah, and even she hadn't riled Tempest's temper the way Constance did.

"Cookie or a piece of this delicious bread? I swear Elvira is worth her weight in gold in the kitchen," Tempest said.

"Be careful about praising the servants or letting them get too friendly with you," Constance chided in a know-it-all voice, as she tilted her chin and looked down at Tempest.

"But I like Elvira and Mama Glory and Washington. They work hard and are good people," Tempest said. "They remind me of our help back home. Fanny and Elvira would have gotten along well. They cook alike, but I have to admit, Elvira's sugar cookies are better than Fanny's were."

Constance rolled her eyes as if to say that wearing britches must addle the brain. "Just beware. It's not good to get familiar with the servants. If you do, they will forget their place."

Tempest bit her lip to keep from starting a full-fledged war about the treatment of servants. It was either rudely change the subject or slap Constance. She decided that rude was the better choice and asked, "So, which do you like best? Red roses or yellow?"

Constance squared her shoulders and answered, "Red, of course. They are so romantic. How can you drink that coffee with no sugar and cream?"

"I like it black and strong. Actually, I liked our campfire coffee best of all. Left over from the night before and heated up is the very best kind." Tempest dipped her cookie into the coffee and rushed the softened sugar treat to her mouth before it dripped onto her shirt.

"It's not ladylike to drink your coffee black or to dip your cookie in it." Clearly Constance was aghast.

"I like cookies with a coffee flavor. Sometimes I pour my coffee over the cinnamon bread and eat it with a spoon. It's wonderful that way. You should try it." Tempest laughed. She'd have to add Constance's last comment to her ever-growing list of unladylike things—britches, riding other than with a sidesaddle, slouching on the settee, and now dipping cookies in coffee. Being a lady sure wasn't much fun.

Constance finished her cookie, daintily dabbed her mouth with a linen napkin, took the last sip of her coffee, and set the cup on the table between them. "I suppose I should be going. You'll tell Micah that I'm so sorry I missed him. I did so want to have a long walk with him and talk about Sally."

"I'll tell Washington. Hopefully, I won't even see Micah today," Tempest said.

"Why?"

"We argue a lot," Tempest said. She wasn't about to tell Constance that when they were alone, they also talked about Constance's cousin, Sally, murdering Micah's father.

Constance stood up and glared down at Tempest. "You are a horrible excuse for a woman, Tempest. Wearing men's clothing will never get you a husband. And your manners leave even more to be desired than your dress. I can't imagine you being a sister to the lovely Delia and Fairlee."

Tempest stood up slowly. She could almost hear her mother's voice whispering in her ear to be nice, or else Constance would have won the battle. "Let me show you to the door. Give Edith my warm regards, and tell her that she is fortunate to have such a loving niece to stand by her."

Constance marched across the foyer and didn't even look at Washington when he opened the door. She stomped all the way to her carriage and slung herself into the seat. She'd been bested and couldn't even whine about it, because the only words from Tempest's mouth had been kind ones.

Tempest waited until she was gone and downed another whole cup of lukewarm black coffee to get the bad taste out of her mouth. Nothing had ever been as wickedly hard in her whole life as being nice to that woman. She would rather have slapped her for her hateful remarks or else poisoned her coffee.

"What's got you in a mood?" Micah asked from the doorway.

She looked across the room at him. His hair was combed back, and his eyes glittered with mischief. She wanted to kiss him or shoot him. Either one would ease the tension in her heart.

"I've been taking care of you again. That would put a nun in a bad mood. How long have you been in the house, and how did you get in? I figured Constance could ferret you out by smell," she smarted off.

Micah grinned. "That's not very . . ."

She put up both palms. "Don't say it. I don't care if I'm not ladylike. I don't care what anyone thinks of me wearing pants and riding a horse the right way. I don't even care if they don't like the way I drink my coffee. I'm me. Take me or leave me. It doesn't really matter."

His grin widened. "Today I'll take you. You saved me from an hour with Constance. That's being a real friend."

"Well, thank you for noticing. Now I'm going into the office to do paperwork. If she comes back, you are on your own."

Her arm brushed against his on her way out the door, and he reached out to touch her elbow. His hand was warm even through her shirt, and sparks flew around them that had little to do with anger or arguments.

"If she comes back, I'm running away. Thanks, Tempie," he said softly as he brought her hand up to his lips and brushed a kiss across her fingertips.

He was taken aback by what the kiss caused deep inside his heart.

She shoved her hand into her pocket and hoped it didn't set the fabric on fire.

"You are welcome, but don't make a habit of leaving me with that woman. I don't like her, and she sure doesn't like me. Being nice to her about killed me," Tempest threw over her shoulder as she headed for the office. She hoped she could keep her mind about her well enough to get the figures into the ledger that afternoon. Maybe she should go on back to Louisiana. She could fight off Matthew Cheval. She wasn't so sure about Micah Burnet.

He followed her into the study and propped a hip on the arm of a chair, while she organized papers and took out a sheet to make a list before setting it down permanently in the ledger book.

She wished he'd go on about his business and leave her to her ledgers, but something seemed to hold him there. Cherish brought in another tray with coffee and cookies and set it on the table. Micah poured himself a cup and eased down into the comfortable chair as if he were waiting for her to say something.

Tempest sat behind the desk, not feeling comfortable in his chair when he was in the room, but she couldn't very well spread out her work on the floor. She opened the ledger to the pages she'd worked on the week before. Surely he would leave if she ignored him and set about her work.

He finished his coffee and poured another cup.

She sighed.

Finally he spoke. "I've got to tell Isaac and Tyrell. They think I should be all broken up and feel the way they would if they lost Fairlee or Delia. They don't understand."

"Then tell them," she said.

"Would you tell your sisters if you'd been the cause of your father or mother's death?"

The room went so still, she could hear the robins singing outside the window and the chatter of squirrels in the pecan trees. The beat of her heart sounded like thumping drums, and she could almost hear her blood whooshing through her veins. Could she tell Fairlee and Delia such a thing?

"I don't think I could. But it would eat holes in my heart not to be able to share that with them," she answered honestly.

He nodded. "That's exactly where I am."

"Maybe you need to forgive Sally before you can tell anyone," Tempest said.

"I can't. I've tried, but I can't. Could you?"

Tempest shook her head so hard that several strands of hair came loose and floated around her face. "Never, but I do pity her."

"Why? Because she's dead?" Micah asked.

"No, that's not it. I'm not sure I can put it into words, especially to you," Tempest said.

"Pretend I'm Delia, then, and tell me why you pity Sally. She shot and killed my father for no reason except to protect her own cheating hide," Micah said.

"Okay, but remember, you asked for it," Tempest said. "Women are just as smart as men, but they can't do the things men do because of society. We have to be wives and mothers and put up with whatever abuse men deal out to us. So it's no wonder Sally decided to go after someone with money and a kind heart. That meant she would be taken care of, and you aren't a mean person, so she wouldn't be abused."

"I'd never hit or beat a woman," he said through gritted teeth.

"Sally knew that."

"Even if she didn't love me like she did Frank, why was she seeing him on the sly and in my parents' cabin? That was adding insult to injury."

"A woman can give her heart to one man and marry another for security."

"Are you on her side or mine?"

"Neither. I'm neutral. She should have been honest and told you about Frank. She should have married him and endured the lifestyle he offered. There's a lot of things she should have done, and she should not have shot your father. I'm just saying that I pity the woman for her bad choices, even though I didn't like her."

Micah nodded slowly. "I think I understand what you're saying. I'm not ready to forgive her, though."

"You may never be ready, or it might come about slowly. Time is the only thing that will take care of it, and when it's time to tell your brothers, it'll be natural and easy. Until then, put yourself in their shoes, and understand that they are only wanting to help you," she said.

"Most of the time folks tend to give a person wings and a halo when they die. Is that because of the old adage of not speaking ill of the dead?" He didn't expect an answer but was thinking aloud.

Tempest giggled. "If I remember right, you outlaws gave us Lavalle sisters wings and halos, and we were still living and deserved them less than any females on earth."

Micah shot her a look. "Looks can be deceiving," he said.

"Now that we've got that settled, you can either help me or get out of here so I can get this done. As it is, I'm an hour behind because I had to entertain your woman," Tempest said.

His mouth set in a line so tight that his lips were barely visible. "Don't call Constance my woman. I'll never trust another woman, especially not a Duval."

Tempest bit back a smile. Now they were on familiar territory. "Okay, then, you pull up a chair and help me sort through these scraps of paper you've written on. While you categorize them, I'll start listing."

He pulled a straight chair from in front of the desk and picked up the stack of paper. Cottonseed went into the debit pile along with the receipt for bolts of calico for the servants' summer dresses. Money from three bales of last fall's cotton shipped to Jackson went into the credit pile.

She drew a line down the middle of a sheet of paper and began to list the expenditures on one side and the profits on the other. The former was outweighing the latter that week, but it was spring, and that wasn't uncommon. Come fall when the crops came in, it would reverse. At least it always had on her Uncle Jonathan's plantation.

"Why do you make extra work for yourself? You could just enter these into the ledger," he said.

"I like to cross-check the amounts against the sales slips first. Then, when I transfer the totals to the ledger, I cross-check everything again. That way, when you balance your columns at the end of each month, it will be an hour-long, easy job instead of a day-long, pull-your-hair-out job."

He finished and stood up. "I really don't care how you do it. I'm just glad for the help. I'm going back out to see how Ben is coming along with the planting. Have you met our foreman?"

"Several times. He's been in and out of our house. I mean Delia's house. Delia really likes him."

"He's a good man. Been with us for ten years as foreman. His father worked for us in that capacity before he died. We're lucky to have Benjamin."

"Is he married?"

"No, why? You interested? Or are you going to do that woman thing and play matchmaker?" Micah felt as if cold water had been splashed on him.

Tempest had a wicked look in her dark blue eyes. "Only person I know trying to find a husband is Constance, and I wouldn't do that to my worst enemy."

Micah headed for the door. "I'll warn Ben."

"You do that. Tell him to steer clear of that woman. She's pure poison."

Tempest bent her head to her work but cut her eyes at Micah as he left the room. He was a very handsome, very caring man. No wonder both Sally and Constance thought he'd be a good catch.

When she finished making all the entries, she put the ledger away and settled her hat on her head. Washington sent someone to bring her horse around to the front and waited with her on the front porch.

"Miss Tempest, I worry about you riding alone. You should have an escort," he said.

Tempest patted him on the arm. "I can take care of myself, Washington. But thanks for caring."

"We all like having your sisters and you on the plantation. Miss Delia done made Mister Tyrell whistle again. And Mister Isaac is smiling more these days. Too bad about Miss Sally, but sometimes God, He has a plan."

The stable hand brought her horse, and she mounted gracefully. "Yes, He does. Sometimes I'm glad I don't know what He has in store for us, though."

"Ain't that the truth?" Washington's grin showed off beautiful white, even teeth.

Her ride scared up a couple of rabbits and a raccoon, but

other than that it was just the birds singing, the field hands harmonizing in an old spiritual as they planted cottonseed, and the distant baying of a hound dog. She left her horse in the stable at Tyrell's and went into the house by the back door and up the stairs to her bedroom, where she threw off her britches, boots, and shirt. She slipped a cotton day dress over her head and buttoned it up the front. Dark blue flowers were scattered over a background of a lighter shade, almost the exact same color as the summer sky. She took down her hair and brushed all the tangles out before braiding it into two long ropes and wrapping them around her head like a crown.

She found Delia in the kitchen talking to Mama Glory and Manny about supper. Her eldest sister was the tallest of the three girls. Aunt Rachel said each successive Lavalle girl got shorter, had curlier hair, and boasted darker blue eyes. Delia was proof. She had pale blue eyes and was five feet six inches tall.

"Well, hello. I understand you had a visitor over at Micah's and played the hostess," Delia said.

Mama Glory frowned and wiped her hands on a white bibbed apron.

"Constance must have stopped by here on her way home." Tempest tried to keep the ice from her voice.

"She did. I invited her to Sunday dinner. Poor dear. There she is, nineteen years old and about to become an old maid."

"I'm nineteen, and I sure don't consider myself about to become an old maid," Tempest said.

"Well, you are. Lots of girls are married at sixteen and seventeen and have families by our age."

"You were past twenty," Tempest argued.

"And what did Aunt Rachel say?"

"Okay, you win," Tempest sighed.

Delia went on, "It seems that with all you two have in common, you could become friends, but she says she feels that you don't like her. She actually wept about it, Tempest." Delia's blue eyes were accusing.

Tempest picked up a cold biscuit and nibbled on the edges. "Poor thing. And is she coming to Sunday dinner?"

"Oh, yes. She was eager for company. It's not easy for her. Sally was like a sister to her, but that won't make the next year any easier. There she is, in her prime for finding a husband, and she's in mourning for a year. It's the right and proper thing to do, since they were so very close, but see it in her light. She'll be twenty by the time the year is over," Delia said.

"We weren't ready to put you in the attic," Tempest answered.

"I'm a Lavalle. We're different. This is Constance. She needs and wants a husband, children, stability," Delia said.

"That mean you're going to throw Micah into the pen with her?" Tempest asked.

Mama Glory gasped.

"Gracious, no! I was thinking about Ben," Delia said. "It would be nice to invite him to Sunday dinner too. Micah is still mourning for Sally."

Tempest smiled. "What did Benjamin ever do to you?"

Delia set her jaw. Tempest had seen her do it a thousand times, and that was only a minor exaggeration. When Delia had wanted them all to go to Texas and Fairlee had disagreed, she'd gotten that expression on her face, and they'd all gone to Texas. When she'd wanted to marry Tyrell and they'd argued, there was that expression again. When she looked like that it meant that she intended to have her way. Well, Tempest wasn't giving in to her even if she did feel as if she was being squeezed between a boulder and a hard place.

"Constance is right. I don't like her," Tempest confessed.

"And why is that?" Delia asked.

She couldn't tell part of the story without telling all of it, and she was sworn to secrecy. "Mama Glory, why don't *you* like her?" she asked instead.

"Woman is kin to Miss Sally. They was cut from the same bolt of sorry cotton. Vincent Duval had two brothers. One was Miss Sally's daddy, and he's gone on, and it's not right to speak ill of the dead, so I ain't sayin' a word except that he wasn't Mister Vincent. Hard work and him didn't get along too good. The other is Miss Constance's daddy, and he's still livin' down in Jackson, and he ain't much better than Sally's daddy was."

Tempest's curiosity was piqued. "Go on."

"I done said enough. Miss Constance is comin' to dinner on Sunday with the whole family. Maybe she's not like her momma."

Delia heard the baby cry and hurried up the back staircase.

"What was her momma like?" Tempest pushed on.

"Like Miss Constance and Miss Sally. Sisters, them women were. And that's all I'm sayin'. It's not my place to tell tales." Mama Glory snapped her mouth shut.

Tempest leaned across the table. "I won't breathe a word of what you say."

Mama Glory shook her head. "No. I can't say nothin' else. Just watch that woman. She's like her momma. Miss Delia is too good to see it, but you . . ."

Tempest smiled. "So I'm not as good as Delia?"

Mama Glory shook her finger at Tempest. "Ain't nobody, man or woman, as good as Miss Delia. But you? Ain't nobody goin' to fool you, girl. Now get on about your business, and keep your eyes open. You can learn a lot that way."

Tempest picked up another biscuit and went out to enjoy the fresh spring air on the front porch.

"Poor old Ben. I'll have to warn him to be careful," she mumbled.

Chapter Five

Delia had moved the place cards so many times that it made Tempest dizzy. The only two that had remained in the same place since the night before were Tyrell's seat at the head of the long dining room table and Delia's to his right. Tempest didn't care where she sat so long as it wasn't next to Constance.

Tempest gave up trying to figure out her sister's plan as Delia played ring-around-the-table with a handful of fancy cards. Leaving Delia to figure out the best possible seating plan in the next ten minutes before all the guests arrived, she headed to the porch to sit in a rocker. She'd barely sat down when Micah rode up and tied his horse to the hitching rail just outside the yard fence.

"What did Mama Glory make today?" he asked as he slumped down in the chair beside Tempest.

"Ham, fried chicken, and roast beef. All three so everyone would have a choice. Delia likes ham on Sunday, but she was afraid there might be those who didn't. Are you aware that Constance is invited, and Delia is matching her with Benjamin?"

"Ben's a big old Irish boy. He can take care of himself. Besides, I don't think Constance would be happy with that arrangement, do you? So, basically, Ben is safe," Micah said.

"You got that right. She's got her sights set on the owner, not the foreman."

"I've got an idea that might stop her nonsense," Micah said.

"It's against the law to shoot her," Tempest whispered.

"You pretended to be a nun and fooled us for a whole week. You reckon you could pretend that you and I are interested in each other?" Micah asked.

Tempest stopped rocking and cocked her head to one side. "I'm not *that* good an actress."

"Please. It won't be but for a little while. Maybe just today. I'll be attentive, and you can be nice for one day."

"I'm not so sure I can. Besides, I already . . . oh, my, they're here." She pointed to the carriage bringing Edith, Vincent, and Constance Duval for dinner.

Micah stood up and offered her his hand. When she took it, that same jolt of electricity that she'd had when he kissed her fingers glued her to the porch. She was glad the Duval women took their time getting out of the carriage. She needed a moment to catch her breath.

"We're the welcoming committee," Micah said.

"Good afternoon. It's good to be here. I hope Mama Glory made her famous ham," Vincent said.

"Yes, she did. Tempie and I were just discussing the menu, and ham is definitely on it. Delia is waiting inside, but the day was so nice, Tempie and I decided to wait on the porch and welcome everyone. Please let me get the door for you. We'll be in as soon as everyone arrives," Micah said.

Constance gave Tempest a look meant to drop her into nothing but a pile of bones inside a lovely pale blue dress, with a wide collar dipping into a deep *V* in the front and back.

"I'd be glad to wait out here with you," Constance said.

"Delia is having such a difficult time with the place cards. I'm sure she'd love to have your advice," Tempest said.

Edith looped her arm through Constance's. "Come along, dear. We are very good at table arrangements. It's a matter of putting people together who have something in common, because there will be several conversations going on all at once, and if one person has no idea how to converse with the guest beside him or her, it becomes quite boring. So let's go help Delia."

Tempest poked Micah's arm once the others were inside. "You jumped that first fence with my help. Now, what are you going to do if she goes in there and redoes the placement so you have to sit beside her?"

"Find an excuse to go home," he said.

An open buggy brought Isaac and Fairlee next. Isaac drove and Fairlee sat beside him. She wore a lovely green dress sprigged with deeper green leaves. It was cut in the same style as Tempest's, with a *V* neckline and a billowing skirt that accentuated her small waist.

"Well, don't you look lovely today," Micah said as he helped Fairlee down from the buggy.

"Thank you," she said.

Isaac was quick to pull Fairlee close to his side. They'd only been married a few months, and he was still amazed that she was his wife. They'd fought their mutual attraction tooth, nail, hair, and eyeball to the bitter end, but when they did commit to each other, it had been just as wholeheartedly.

"Miss Tempie, you look like a breath of spring," Isaac said.

"What does that mean, exactly? I've often wondered, because spring can bring some pretty nasty odors and . . ."

"Tempie, say 'thank you' and hush," Fairlee admonished her sister, laughing.

"Thank you and hush," Tempest said with a gleam of mischief in her eyes.

"So are you two coming in or staying out?" Isaac asked.

"We're waiting on Ben. He should be here any minute. He's probably taming that mop of red hair," Micah said.

"Are you talking about me?" Benjamin rounded the side of the house and stepped up onto the porch.

"We were. Now we can all go in together, and Delia can stop being so nervous," Tempest said.

"What's she got to be nervous about? It's just Sunday dinner," Ben said. "We've done this lots of times."

Micah whispered in his ear, and Ben's face went ashen. "You've got to be kiddin' me. I thought she wanted to be a Burnet."

"What?" Fairlee caught the last of the conversation.

Tempest looped her arm in Fairlee's and led her inside. "Nothing. Let's go on inside. It's only a few minutes until we'll be seated. You menfolk will want to gather in the library with Tyrell, I'm sure."

Fairlee set her heels outside the parlor door, where the voices of Delia, Constance, and Edith blended together into a buzz. She locked gazes with Tempest. "You're holding something back, and I can smell a rat a mile away."

"Delia is matchmaking."

Fairlee rolled her dark blue eyes at the ceiling. "Sally's only been gone a few weeks. Micah isn't ready to make another commitment."

Tempest's head bobbed up and down the whole time

Fairlee was whispering. "I told her that. She's not trying to match Constance with Micah. It's Ben."

Fairlee clamped a hand over her mouth. "You're joking."

"Nope. She feels so sorry for Constance because she's about to be an old maid, and she wants to help her find happiness. But—get this—Constance is trying to wrangle a way into Micah's house and bed."

"Tempest Lavalle!"

"It's the truth. She's left no doubt in my mind what she's up to, and . . ."

Fairlee's expression went dead serious. "I trust your judgment. But Ben?"

"What about Ben?" Micah asked from the doorway as the three men came inside and started toward the library to join Tyrell and Vincent.

"I hear he's sitting beside Constance," Fairlee said.

Ben's face turned as red as his hair. "I wouldn't disappoint Miss Delia for anything, so I'll get through the dinner. But I've got a lady friend already."

"Oh? Who is this friend?" Tempest raised an eyebrow.

"It's a secret," Ben said with a chuckle.

Tyrell came out of the library just as the clock struck one. "That means it's time for dinner. Delia, shall we go first?" He poked his head in the door and motioned for his wife.

"Of course," she said. She'd never liked formality, but sometimes it was nice to get dressed up for Sunday dinner and have company. She took Tyrell's arm and motioned for Edith and Vincent to follow. Fairlee and Isaac fell in behind the older couple.

Constance smiled brightly, winked, and looped her arm through Tempest's. "Shall we? I'm sure those two strong men can find their way from the parlor to the kitchen, aren't you?"

Tempest was speechless.

Ben grinned.

Micah shook his head slowly.

"Time to bury the hatchet. We got off on the wrong foot. I was upset over my dear Sally, and I lashed out at you. It was all my fault. Forgive me?" Constance whispered.

Tempest smiled. "Of course."

Tempest wasn't one to hold a grudge forever, but forgiving wasn't the same as trusting.

Delia looked up from the dining table where she and the rest of the party waited behind their chairs. She raised an eyebrow at Tempest, who simply winked.

Delia didn't know what was going on, but everyone was waiting to be seated, so she said, "Constance, your place is here beside me, right across the table from Tempest. Ben, you'll be sitting on the other side of Constance. Micah, you are to Tyrell's left, and, Tempest, you'll be between him and Fairlee."

"Good. Fairlee and I can catch up on the new house construction," Tempest said.

She and Constance parted company at the head of the table, with Constance going to the right and Tempest to the left. Had the woman really had a change of heart when she figured out that the only female neighbors anywhere close to her age could easily ignore her for the next year?

Tempest didn't think for one minute that Constance was sincere. What she did think was that the woman had figured out another way to get inside the family and next to Micah. And that made Tempest very jealous and then angry for being jealous.

"What happened?" Micah whispered from the side of his mouth after Vincent had delivered a long grace.

"Later," Tempest said.

Bowls of steamy hot potato soup were set in front of the guests to begin the meal. Platters of hot, yeasty rolls were scattered down the middle of the table. Water goblets were filled. The dining room was soon buzzing with conversations. Micah and Tyrell discussed the price of cottonseed and speculated on the fall crop. Ben, Vincent, and Isaac were deep into a conversation about the pros and cons of planting tobacco.

Constance looked across the table at Tempest and Fairlee. "So, tell me about the new house. I can't think of anything more exciting than having a new home exactly the way you want it."

"It's about the size of Micah's place and laid out pretty much the same as that one and this one. Big old shady porch for the evenings. Faces east so we can watch the sun come up from our balcony. You'll have to come and see the progress," Fairlee said.

"I would love to do that. What day would be best? I'm free anytime that's good for you except Friday. I usually help Aunt Edith with her flower garden on that day," Constance said. "Would you be interested in some rose clippings for your new place? I'll bring some gallon jars to start them under, the way my momma taught me, and the clippings, if you know where you'd like to put them."

"I've got gallon jars in the barn, and yes . . ."

Constance held up a palm. "Don't thank us. You know the roses won't live if you say thank you. It's a bad omen."

"When it comes to growing roses, I'm all thumbs, so I'll not say the words and jinx the flowers," Fairlee said. "Do you have any yellow ones like the ones that grow wild in Delia's yard?"

"No, I'm afraid not. But Aunt Edith does have some lovely specimens that I could get going for you." Constance turned to compliment her hostess. "Delia, this is wonderful soup. I must have your recipe. What's giving it that smoky flavor?"

"Bacon. Mama Glory fries bacon and crumbles it into the soup and adds a bit of clotted cream just before she serves it," Delia said.

"Well, it's truly wonderful," Constance said.

Tempest waited for the gloves to come off and the barbs to begin, but they didn't. By the time they'd finished dinner, she was almost convinced that Constance Duval had truly not been herself the day of Sally's funeral and the weeks following.

She was a pretty young woman even in her black mourning dress. Her eyes were lively that day and her brown hair styled high on top of her head. In a year, when the official mourning season was over, she'd be lovely wearing springtime colors. The young men of Greenville, Mississippi, would be flocking to the spring picnic at the Duval plantation to get a chance to dance with her.

Maybe even Micah, once he sees the softer side of Constance. He might learn to like her in a year, especially when he sees her in this light.

Another burst of jealousy shot through Tempest. She shook her head and wondered what was the matter with her. She shouldn't be jealous. Micah could court whomsoever he pleased. She should be matchmaking and trying to get them together instead of fighting to keep them apart.

"Whatever are you thinking about?" Delia asked her.

Tempest was so busy arguing with her conscience that she didn't hear her sister.

"Tempie?" Delia said sternly.

She looked up from her potato soup with a question in her eyes.

"I was talking to you," Delia said.

Tempest looked from her to Constance, who shrugged.

"I asked what you were thinking about," Delia said.

"Why?"

"Your expression looked as if you were having a lively conversation with yourself. It kept changing from angry to amused," Constance said.

"I was thinking about those Indians who'd kidnapped little Hannah Marie Smith, and then I was thinking about how angry I'd be if anyone ever hurt Etta Ruth, and then I started remembering Etta's sweet smiles," Tempest improvised. She *had* been thinking about those very things the day before.

"What Indians?" Constance asked.

"You tell her, Delia. You were the brave one who stood up to that Indian chief and bartered for that little girl," Tempest said.

The whole table went silent.

"It's a bit of a story," Delia said.

"Entertain us, please," Edith said. "If I have to hear about cotton and tobacco much longer, I'm going to fall asleep at the table."

"Go ahead. I love that story. I think it's when I first realized how much I loved you." Tyrell touched Delia's shoulder.

Delia laid her spoon down and started. "On our way back from the Alamo, we came upon an Indian village. It was in a clearing, and they'd seen us, so we didn't have much choice but to go right on through it. Tyrell told us to keep our eyes open and make a run for it if the arrows or bullets starting flying. I wanted to make a run for it, but we rode straight ahead single file, with Tyrell first and then me, Isaac, Fairlee, Tempest, and Micah bringing up the rear."

Constance threw a hand over her breast and gasped. "What happened?"

"We didn't even make it to the edge of the village before a bunch of braves rode out to meet us. They lined up crosswise in a row to show us how strong they were and to dare us to try to get through them. We lined up in front of them the same way to show them they didn't scare us one bit," Delia said.

"Did they scare you?" Constance asked.

"They made me madder than they actually frightened me. I was tired, and they were keeping me from getting home. Tyrell told them that we were travelers, not warriors, and just wanted to ride to the other side of their encampment. One of the young men translated to the fellow who seemed to be in charge, and he told us we'd have to follow them to Chief Running Deer, who'd talk to us some more. I didn't want to talk. I wanted to get the day's ride done and find a place to rest," Delia said.

"But she was brave." Tyrell smiled proudly.

Delia smiled back. "Didn't have much choice when they surrounded us and forced us to the chief's teepee. Tyrell went in first, and we all followed. The chief sat on a pile of fur pelts. He motioned for us to sit. And Tyrell told him that we honored him as the chief of his people and didn't want to hurt anyone, that we were on the way home from a long journey. And that's when the trouble began. He said that everyone could pass through safely if he could have me."

Edith gasped at that. "Oh, my!"

"I have to admit, I got a little scared then, but it didn't take me long to get mad all over again when Tyrell told them that I was his wife but that I was good-for-nothing. He even said that I burned the food and that no self-respecting brave would want me."

Tempest giggled at the memory. "And such fire shot from her eyes, I thought that teepee would go up in flames."

Micah chuckled. "Seems the chief wanted her for a wife for his son."

Delia shivered, remembering the way she had felt that day. "He said that his son would like the color of my eyes and that our children would have blue eyes and they would be honored in the tribe."

"Are blue eyes honored in the tribe?" Ben asked.

"I have no idea, but Tyrell said that he couldn't give up his wife, and he offered some other gift for the tribe's hospitality. I was so nervous, I could hardly sit still. And in those days, I certainly didn't want to be Tyrell's wife! I was going to pitch a fit, but then a little girl rushed into the tent. That old chief looked exactly the way Momma did back when we were kids and she was exasperated with us. The child said that the other children were hitting her again and wouldn't stop and that she wanted her momma. She had blue eyes and a tangled mess of blond hair hanging in her eyes. After taking one look at me, she ran to my side and begged me to help her. She said she wanted to go home. I asked who she was, and the chief said that women didn't speak unless they were spoken to and for Sky Eyes to go and find her father."

"Had they kidnapped that little girl?" Edith asked.

"Yes, they had, though they said that they had simply found her, and that if a wife was not found for his son, then the little girl would become his wife when she was old enough, because the son wanted a wife with blue eyes. He had seen a vision in some ceremony when he became a man, and in it he had a blue-eyed wife."

"That's horrible," Constance said.

"That's what I thought too. Tyrell told the chief that I couldn't have children and that I liked the child. He told the translator to ask the chief if he could buy the little girl, but the chief said no, but I could be the son's wife and thus be her mother."

Tempest pointed at Tyrell. "Remember what you said then?"

Tyrell grinned. "I planned to offer him you or Fairlee instead of Delia. And you told me that I wouldn't dare."

"And the old chief told me to be quiet," Tempest remembered.

"Brave old fool, wasn't he?" Ben laughed.

"Stupid is more like it," Delia said. "Tempest shoved her finger under his nose and told him not to talk to her like that. She said she wasn't a bag of sugar that he could sell anytime he wanted, and the chief said he didn't want her because she was too mean."

"He got that right," Micah said.

Constance's eyes lit up, and a smile toyed at the corners of her mouth when Micah made that comment.

"Well, he wasn't going to tell me to be quiet, and he wasn't taking Delia away from us, either. I'd have shot him and then started on his braves before that happened," Tempest said.

"Then Tyrell did try to sell me instead of Delia. We should have known that they were destined to be together even back then," Fairlee said.

Delia picked up the story again. "But the chief didn't want her either. So I told him that I would kill his son in his sleep. I lied and said that I loved my husband and I'd rather be dead than have another husband. Finally he said that he believed me and told Isaac, Tyrell, and Micah that they hadn't done well when they got us, and he said they would have done better to come to the Indians for wives because they trained their women better than the white man did. But he had to have a present to let us ride across the land."

"What did you give them?" Ben asked.

"I told Tyrell to talk fast and hard because I was taking the child with me. The chief said that the girl was worthless and only caused trouble and that I would be better off with a nice Indian child. It took a while, but we finally traded our pack horse and everything on it for the child and safe passage. I tried to negotiate a better deal, saying he'd already told us that the girl was worthless, but he said that the supplies and Tyrell's gun would purchase us the girl. The horse bought us safe passage through his territory, and I was never, ever to tell anyone that he had bargained with a woman. It would be a blow to his pride," Delia told them.

"And you gave up your supplies? How did you survive?" Constance asked.

"Tyrell gave up everything. I swear, Tempest probably would have gone toe-to-toe with him over the food, but I wanted that child out of there. But the adventure wasn't over yet. We mounted up, and Tyrell handed the dirty little girl up to me. And we started out of the camp. I was about to breathe easily when this Indian brave rode up and started having a fit. He sent for the man who'd been translating, and, let me tell you, the five minutes that we waited lasted three days past eternity. Then along came the translator, and he showed the brave what a fine horse and supplies and gun they'd traded for. He reminded him that white girls with blue eyes were always there for the taking and that maybe the next one would be old enough to be his wife. At least that's what I got from all the gesturing and talk. Finally the brave picked up the horse's reins and led it back toward his father's teepee. And the translator told us to go in a hurry, that the brave was finally satisfied."

Tyrell picked up the story when Delia stopped for a sip of water. "But Delia couldn't keep her mouth shut. If I remember the words right, she said, 'Well, thank God for that. We wouldn't want him to be upset.' The translator told me that white women would be the fall of the white man's world if they didn't learn their place. He offered for me to leave her with him, and he'd teach her to be quiet. He said a strong green switch was good to train a woman who spoke when she shouldn't."

"Remember what you told him?" Tempest asked.

Tyrell nodded. "I said I'd take his advice and beat her when we got home," Tyrell said.

"And what did she say back to you?" Fairlee asked.

" 'You and what army?' " Delia answered.

Everyone around the table laughed.

"What happened then?" Edith asked.

"He said for Tyrell to beat me hard, every day for a week, and Tyrell just nodded. He knew he was in enough hot water. Anyway, we cleaned Hannah up, and you'll never believe it, but in the next town we stopped in, we found her parents. They were so excited that they gave us supplies and a new pack animal. But I really kind of wanted to keep Hannah," Delia said.

"Remember what we said about the Indians and our habits?" Fairlee said.

"What habits?" Constance asked.

"That's a story for another time," Delia said. She motioned to Manny, who removed their soup bowls. As soon as they were gone, dishes and platters of food were set down along the middle of the table.

"This looks so good. Listening to that story built up an appetite I haven't had in weeks," Constance said.

"Poor dear has been so blue since Sally's death that she hasn't eaten enough to keep body and soul together," Edith said.

Delia shot a look across the table at Tempest that said she'd better not say one smart word about Edith's comment. "Well, I'm glad that my story brought back your appetite."

"You should have been there. Delia was a force, let me tell you," Tempest said.

Delia smiled.

"Sounds like you were pretty brave too. I never could have talked to that chief like that," Constance said.

Something didn't feel right to Tempest. No one made such an abrupt change of character in such a short time, but she would give Constance the benefit of the doubt. At least until the woman showed her original true colors.

"Sure, you could. It was either pretend to be mean or have to be a wife to that ill-tempered son of his," Tempest said.

"You weren't pretending," Micah said. "You *are* mean."

Constance's eyes glittered when she looked across the table at Micah.

Chapter Six

Micah sat with his back against the big oak tree and fanned his straw hat to stir a little breeze. The old folks said that March always came in like a lion and went out like a lamb. But it had pushed February out of the picture very quietly without much pomp, and it was about to give up the ghost and let April come on in without much fanfare except for one hot day. If the day was any indication of what summer was going to be like, they could get ready for a real scorcher that year. They needed rain, but so far the spring had been stingy with its moisture.

He heard hoofbeats and looked up from his shady place to see Constance Duval riding across the land toward Fairlee and Isaac's place. He remembered hearing them talking about planting roses at the new house site. She hadn't noticed him, and if his luck held and she kept riding on past, he'd steer clear of the place for the rest of the day. The woman and her tears made him nervous. He'd grown used to Tempest, who spoke her mind even if it aggravated a saint into swearing.

Ben said Constance had been very nice to him during Sunday dinner and while dessert was served had asked him how long he'd worked for the Burnet family. But she hadn't flirted or led him to believe she'd be interested in anything other than dinner-table conversation. Maybe he and Tempest had both gotten a wrong first impression.

Micah had sure enough gotten the wrong first impression of the Lavalle sisters. First they had appeared to be nuns, then they didn't, and he hadn't really liked them either way. He'd learned to love Delia and Fairlee like real sisters, but it hadn't happened that first morning when they'd been released from jail to escort the sisters away from the Alamo to safety. It hadn't happened along the trail, either, but once two of them married Tyrell and Isaac, he'd seen another side of the Lavalles. If Tempest ever got married, would he learn to like her too?

The idea of her being another man's wife sent a jealous streak to jab at his heart, and that confused him. He tried to picture her sitting beside someone in church, building a home and having children with another man, but every single vision just made him angrier.

He didn't even need to shut his eyes to see a vision of the Lavalle sisters wearing their black habits and riding in the back of the wagon. He'd respected them as nuns. Well, all but Tempest, who'd giggled too much and had too much mischief in her eyes to be a nun. Then the next week they'd come down the hotel stairs all dressed in britches and boots, ready to ride horses and shoot guns like a man. His first impression of them that day had been one of pure disgust. Maybe that's where he was with Constance. He'd been disgusted with her actions at Sally's death. And maybe he should give her a second chance, since she'd been so sweet and kind at Sunday dinner.

His train of thought was broken by the noise of another horse coming across the land at a fast speed. He expected to look up and see Ben hunting him down with a problem to be solved and was surprised when it turned out to be Tempest, riding like a bat set loose from the bowels of Hades. She had the reins in one hand and held her hat on with the other. He stuck his forefingers into his mouth and whistled as loudly as he could.

Tempest heard the shrill whistle a minute before her horse came to a screeching halt. If she hadn't held on for dear life, she would have been tossed head over boot heels right over the animal's head. Whoever had pulled a stunt like that was about to endure a tongue-lashing more painful than any whipping he'd had the misfortune to be on the other end of a switch from. Her horse had been trained to come to her at a whistle like that, so she couldn't blame him for stopping to see why she was whistling when they were speeding toward Fairlee's house.

She dismounted and looked all around, finally spotting Micah waving his hat from the edge of a copse of trees. She waved back and started in that direction. Three months before, when she'd arrived at the Burnet-Fannin plantation, she'd have thought someone was crazier than an outhouse rat if they'd said she and Micah would someday strike up a friendship. But there she was, eager to see him and pass a little time with him.

"What are you doing out here, and why'd you spook my horse like that?" she said when she drew close enough to yell at him.

He put a finger over his mouth and pointed toward Fairlee's cabin and the rider dismounting there.

"Constance," he mouthed dramatically.

She nodded and put some extra speed into her step. By the time she reached him, he was sitting down again with his back to the oak tree. He didn't offer to jump up like a paramour might, but rather patted the ground beside him. "Sit a spell. Constance is up there at Fairlee's. I guess they're planting roses. You might want to linger unless you want to have another one of them catfights."

"Are *you* hiding?" She sat down and braced her back against the same enormous tree trunk.

He nodded and commenced fanning again. "I am until you tell me what was going on at the dinner table on Sunday. Seeing Constance was like meeting two different women. One was at the funeral, and another one came to Sunday dinner. I didn't like the first one, but the second wasn't too bad."

"Oh?" Tempest asked.

"Not romantically. I just liked her better than the other one. She was kind of sweet at Sunday dinner. Even Ben mentioned that, if he wasn't involved with another woman, he might be interested."

Tempest drew her dark eyebrows down in a serious frown. "That's what I wanted to talk to you about. Constance apologized to me for her tacky behavior and blamed it all on Sally's death. People do act weird when someone close to them dies, so maybe I misjudged her. I'd be out of my mind if Delia or Fairlee died. I should go on up to Fairlee's and help plant roses. I'm thinking we might be able to abide each other's company without baring our claws, if she stays as nice as she was on Sunday."

"Sit with me a while," Micah said.

"The shade does feel good," she said.

He fanned her face with his hat and said, "Tell me about

your parents. We never did talk about them. I met your father, and he seemed like a good man, but it was a very brief meeting. We did our business, and he disappeared. Of course, I could have strangled him for letting us believe you were nuns."

"Would you have taken on the job of seeing us home if you'd known we were just three sisters and not holy women?" she asked. That breeze he created with his hat felt so good that she could have sat there until she was old and gray.

"At that time we were all going stir-crazy in that jail cell. Three of us big men in one little cell without room to gripe at a cat without getting hair in our mouths," he said.

She giggled. "I hadn't ever heard that expression before."

"It's not funny. It was the truth. It was pretty tight quarters. What was your father like when he wasn't worried about his daughters?" Micah asked.

"Mother and Father were both passionate in whatever they did. Father was a military man through and through, and he loved it. He liked the travel and seeing new places. Mother didn't, so she stayed home on the plantation that Father and Uncle Jonathan shared. She said we girls should have roots. Father would rather have given us wings, so he taught us all the things that fathers teach their sons. They were always so glad to see each other when he came home between duty postings. But she was also always glad to see him go," Tempest answered.

"Why?"

"Because they argued. A lot! The first few days would be wonderful. He'd spend lots of time with her and us. We'd have picnics if it was in the spring or summer or even early fall. If it was winter, we'd go on long rides in the carriage, and he'd bundle us girls up in quilts. Sometimes he'd take us all out for 'training sessions,' and Mother hated that. She said we were girls, not boys. But I'm glad, because we got the best of both worlds. She taught us to be ladies. He taught us to survive. But after a few weeks of his being there twenty-four hours every day, Mother was ready to have her routine back. I'm glad she was already gone when he was killed at the Alamo, though. I'm not sure she could have survived knowing that he'd never come back to her. She loved him so much."

Micah let that sink in before saying, "Fairlee and Delia act like they would never want to be parted from their husbands."

"I guess they got that part from Aunt Rachel. She was better at the everyday relationship than Mother, but I have no complaints about the way I was raised. It was a good life, and I loved them all."

"All?"

"Sure. Mother. Father. Uncle Jonathan and Aunt Rachel. Fanny used to say that, over in her native country, they said it takes a village to raise a child. I'm living proof of that. Without all four, I'm sure I wouldn't be the person I am today."

Micah nodded seriously. "I guess me and Isaac and Tyrell were about the same. Only we had two houses. When we were little we had four people raising us too.

"Well, I expect I'd best get on about my business. I just stopped for a few minutes in the shade to cool off. See you Friday?"

She nodded, hating to see the hat-making breeze leave. "I'll be there, and I would be very happy if Cherish made up some of that cinnamon bread. She does such a good job with that. Someday she's going to be as good a cook as Elvira. You notice how giddy she gets when Jeremiah comes around? I think they might be flirting." Tempest grinned.

Micah mounted his horse and looked down at her sitting against the tree. "I like the way you Lavalle women treat the servants."

"Mother put us in Fanny's care pretty often. We grew up knowing they were servants, but we never thought of them as slaves or referred to them as that, either. Mother would have punished us for being rude," Tempest said.

"She was a wise woman." Micah rode off through the trees toward the other side of the plantation. If someone had told him three months before that he'd be sitting talking to Tempie Lavalle like a friend, he'd have thought the speaker had brain fever. Knowing that she was coming to live with Delia had been a major factor in his proposal to Sally. He hadn't wanted Delia and Fairlee to try to matchmake him and Tempie. That woman was too much of a handful for him. Friendship was proving to be really nice, but the thought of anything more gave him hives.

Constance planted the last rose cutting in the soil and set a gallon jug over it. She removed her gloves and sat down on the rough wooden bench Isaac had nailed together for Fairlee when she came to check on the house.

Constance had enjoyed planting the flowers and hoped they flourished. Someday she would ask Fairlee, as her sister-in-law, to help her plant cuttings at Micah's house. She envisioned the two of them laughing and talking as they set out roses and lilacs. In her daydream Micah and Isaac came home and rushed to the backyard to check on their wives. By then Fairlee might have a new babe in her arms, and Constance would be hoping for a child with Micah's light brown eyes.

"Are you gathering wool?" Fairlee asked as she handed Constance a glass of lemonade.

"Oh, my, that lemonade looks delicious, and, yes, I was woolgathering. I was thinking about how much Sally would have loved this day and how much she would have enjoyed having you for a sister," Constance lied.

Fairlee sat down beside her. "It was such a shame about Sally. And she went so fast. We are all so very lucky that whatever she had didn't become widespread. That was a miracle."

Constance stared up at the clear blue sky. "Yes, it was. We could have all taken sick with whatever it was that killed her." She looked back at Fairlee. "I love the taste of lemons, and you got it just right with the sugar. Not enough to make it sickeningly sweet and yet enough to cut the sour. I've got to be going if I'm to get home in time to clean up for supper. Aunt Edith likes for us to be dressed for the evening meal, even if it's just the three of us."

"I would say thank you for the roses, but I don't want them to die." Fairlee smiled about the jinx.

"That's right. I thought you said Tempest might be coming over today."

"She'd talked about it. I guess she and Delia got busy on the garden plans, and she forgot."

"One more thing. I never did figure out how you three came to have such strange names. Sally and I talked about it and meant to ask you but never got around to it," Constance said.

"Mother just liked the unusual. Delia is the nickname for a Greek goddess. She said the first time she looked at me, she thought of a golden meadow, and that's what Fairlee means. And the first time she laid eyes on Tempest, she knew that girl would be a handful," Fairlee said, laughing.

"That's the truth. Tempest is scary sometimes," Constance said.

"We all are, Constance," Fairlee said seriously.

"Not so much you and Delia. But Tempest is like a big old black storm."

"And that's why I never worry about her," Fairlee said. Was Constance opening the way for her to speak ill about Tempie? Well, it would never happen.

Constance untied the reins of her horse from the hitching post and deftly hoisted herself into the sidesaddle. "Please feel free to come visit me anytime. I'd love to show you which flowers I took those cuttings from."

"We'll have to plan on a day. Maybe I'll bring my sisters with me. They'd love to see Edith's garden and maybe get some ideas," Fairlee said.

"She'd be delighted. Good-bye now." Constance smiled and rode away.

Tempest was dreaming of the days in San Antonio, Texas, that she and her sisters had spent with their father, Captain Robert Lavalle. She awoke right after arguing with him about leaving in the company of three outlaws he'd hired to escort his daughters home. She looked around, half expecting to see him standing in the living room of his house near the Alamo, and ready to fight with him some more. But she was sitting under the oak tree where Micah had left her an hour before. Her horse raised his head from the green grass he'd been nibbling on, and his ears perked up.

"What is it, boy? Is Micah riding back?" she whispered.

But it wasn't Micah who rode past. It was Constance on

her way home. Tempest sat very still, but her horse gave her away when he neighed loudly. Constance turned and saw her, and there was nothing she could do but wave.

Constance pulled the reins to the left and rode up to where Tempest was still sitting. "What are you doing here?"

"I was out exercising my horse and decided to stop and think for a while. It's such a lovely day that I fell asleep," she said. It was mostly the truth, even if every single detail wasn't.

Constance dismounted and reached for her drawstring purse from the saddle horn. "I've been planting roses with Fairlee. If she'll water them properly and do what I told her, she'll have a lovely garden."

"Oh, I'm sure she will," Tempest said. "She wants a garden like Aunt Rachel had in Louisiana."

Constance was almost giddy. She'd wondered how she could get Tempest alone even for a few minutes, and now fate had delivered her right into her hands. Surely the gods intended for her to have Micah Burnet and were helping her to get rid of the only obstacle in her way. By this time next year she would be a sister to Fairlee and Delia. She began to plan immediately how she would console them after the death of their beloved sister, Tempest. But to think of her own house and a husband who doted on her, the way Isaac did Fairlee and Tyrell did Delia, made her almost dance a jig right there under the oak tree.

She fumbled inside the purse and brought out a small handgun that her mother had given her before she left Jackson.

"What are you doing?" Tempest looked around to see if there was a snake or a varmint near.

"I'm getting rid of the competition like I did with Sally," Constance said coldly.

Tempest started to stand up.

Constance pointed the gun at her. "Sit still. I'll make it as painless as possible. Poor Sally didn't have that option."

Tempest glared at her. "I was right from the beginning."

"Yes, you were. I intend to have a Burnet. I would have been glad to marry Isaac, but Fairlee took him from me. That only leaves Micah. I'm not even sorry that I have to shoot you to get him. It's well worth the price. I never did like you, but your sisters won't ever know that. We can comfort one another together. They'll be sorry for me for losing Sally, and I'll be so very sorry for their loss of you."

Tempest sat very still. If she could only keep Constance talking, perhaps she could figure a way out of this predicament. Maybe Micah would ride back and be able to prevent Constance from pulling the trigger.

"What about Sally?" Tempest asked.

"Stupid girl. I told her she was playing with fire, sneaking around with Frank, but they'd been in love since they were kids. Then he came back to Jackson all heartbroken and got himself killed in a barroom fight. She thought she'd lost Micah for good after she killed his father and he ran off to Texas, but he came back, and she was able to work her way back into his heart. Originally Isaac was supposed to be mine, but your sister ruined it all. Too bad. If she hadn't, I wouldn't have to kill you today."

"Why do you want a Burnet? There's lots of men out there who'd love you. Micah is no prize. He's temperamental and speaks his mind," Tempest said.

"I will have him because this place adjoins my Uncle Vincent's plantation. When he and Aunt Edith are gone, I'll inherit it," Constance said.

"Edith and Vincent have two sons. *They* will inherit the land. And you're forgetting about Isaac and Tyrell."

"Don't you use your last breath to think about that, Tempest Lavalle. I took care of Sally with a little poison. I'm taking care of you with a little bullet. They'll never suspect that I killed you. We buried the hatchet on Sunday. I have had a very nice day today with my new sister, Fairlee. When they find your body, they'll think someone killed you for this fine horse I intend to take with me and sell. It worked for Sally, and it will work for me. And about my two male cousins, Uncle Vincent and Aunt Edith will be so very sad when both their sons die, but I'll be there to comfort them just like I will Delia and Fairlee. And, honey, when Aunt Edith and Uncle Vincent are gone, it will be me who has the lion's share. Your sisters will have to take a backseat to me," Constance said sweetly.

"Let's talk about this. Fairlee knows you're riding past here. She'll figure it out. Did I tell you that we three sisters have special powers when it comes to one another?" Tempest started to stand up.

"I've gotten away with everything so far. Fate sent me to you, and it will not fail me. I thought I'd have to be nice a lot longer than this to gain your confidence." Constance pulled the trigger.

Tempest jerked to one side but not fast enough. She saw the ground reaching up to grab her, but she couldn't keep from tumbling. The last thing she remembered before darkness obliterated the sun was Constance's giggles.

Chapter Seven

Strong arms scooped Tempest up, and wind rushed past her face. She opened her eyes slightly to see a big round ball with twinkling lights all around it fading in and out. Was she on her way to eternity? If she was, then all the Sunday-morning preaching she'd heard had been bogus, because her head was pounding and her shoulder ached like it did the first time she'd been thrown from a horse. According to the Good Book there was to be no more pain or suffering after death. She was supposed to die and then wake up in glory with wings and a halo. Or was what Micah had told her the truth, about her halo being nothing but a trick of the light?

A giggle tried to force its way up from her soul, but she was too weary to let it escape. The round ball was bright again, but it was bouncing past her eyes at a breakneck speed. She'd been wrong about the ascension into heaven too. She thought there'd be a bright light and then—boom—she'd fly so fast toward the Pearly Gates that it would take her breath away. This big round ball of light looked a lot like a full moon.

She tried to keep her eyes open and focus on the bright

ball, but they grew heavy, and she slumped against a broad chest. Strange, no one had ever said that a big, strong man would carry her from earth to heaven. Maybe she wasn't headed for heaven after all. Maybe she had spoken her mind one too many times and Saint Peter didn't want such a sassy woman in his court. Perhaps he'd sent her on to the other place, and the devil had her in his arms, speeding toward Hades.

She roused again, but it was an awful effort to open her eyes. The wind was chilly against her face, and she moaned. If Lucifer would just set her down, they could talk about her soul. She'd make a deal with him, remind him that she could stir up more trouble for him than he wanted to think about.

"Won't be long now," a voice said. It sounded like Jules, one of the servants on the plantation. Good grief! Lucifer had sent a servant. He hadn't even come himself. Well, Tempest had no doubt she could talk a servant into giving her another chance. And if she wasn't dead, then Aunt Rachel would take care of her as soon as Jules got her to the house.

Her head throbbed when she tried to remember what had happened, but a small part of the puzzle floated through her memory, and she latched on to it. She'd been exercising her horse and had ridden out to the edge of the plantation. She'd seen Uncle Jonathan talking to Jules at the end of a cotton field and waved at him. Then she passed the cabins where the servants lived and kept riding. When she reached her favorite spot, she'd dismounted and sat down beside a tree. But it didn't look like a tree on the Louisiana plantation. It was more like the big oak at the edge of the copse between Fairlee's cabin and Micah's house.

Evidently her horse had thrown her on the way back home, and Jules had found her beside the road. She had the two plantations mixed up together in her mind. She wondered if it was Jules carrying her or one of the River Bend plantation servants. Whoever it was had started to pant and to pray. She heard him say something to sweet Jesus before the big round ball and twinkling lights up above her became a blur, then ceased to be.

Micah was restless that evening. It must be spring in the air. The night was cool but not so cold that he couldn't sit on the porch. He wished that Isaac and Fairlee would take an evening drive and come visit him, but that was crazy thinking. If he had a new wife like Fairlee, he sure wouldn't want to spend his evening with the brother he'd just seen that afternoon. Besides, Isaac had said they were going to Tyrell and Delia's that evening because Fairlee had made a new dress for Etta Ruth.

"Well, dang it all," Micah swore. He'd sent Jeremiah over there with a note to Isaac about a load of lumber that he'd ordered from Greenville. The courier from the sawmill had left the wood at his house that day instead of taking it on to the cabin.

"It can't be helped now," Micah said aloud. Jeremiah would bring back the note and go on to his cabin, and Micah would deliver the news tomorrow morning.

He sat down in a chair deep in the shadows of the porch and thought about the day. Maybe he would get to know Constance better. She'd seemed nice enough on Sunday, and she was making a real effort to fit in with the families. She didn't send sparks flying around him when he touched her hand like Tempest did. But then, she didn't make him so mad he could chew up pecan tree logs and spit out kindling either.

He stood up and leaned against a porch post. The moon was full and the stars bright that night. Was that why he was in such an antsy mood? A full moon. Springtime. Tomorrow was April 1, so it wouldn't be long until the days were hot and long, which was a good thing, because cotton needed heat to grow well. He made a trip to the far end of the porch and walked around the house. That didn't help. He thought about riding over to Tyrell's and playing with Etta Ruth, but he didn't want to saddle up a horse.

"I want a dozen kids like her, and I don't care if they're all girls or all boys or a nice combination of both," he said into the night.

He sat back down and saw the silhouette of a man running toward the house. Evidently Jeremiah had plans of his own that evening and wanted to be about them for him to run a mile from Isaac's place back home. He was nearing twenty years old and could be interested in taking a wife. Micah had seen him eyeing Cherish on several occasions. If that was the way of things, Micah would give his blessing for sure. Jeremiah was a good, hardworking man, and Cherish was a big help to Elvira in the kitchen. They were both assets to the plantation, and they deserved happiness.

Micah looked up and focused on Jeremiah as he drew closer. It looked as if he were carrying someone or something. Perhaps a small calf. Maybe he'd run across a heifer who'd died giving birth or a wild horse who'd abandoned a colt. That was more likely, since the package in his arms had long dangling limbs like a baby horse.

"Mister Micah, get some help! She's been hurt bad!" Jeremiah yelled from fifty yards out, and he kept running.

"What is it?" Micah called back, watching as the man got closer and closer.

"It's Miss Tempest. There's blood on her shirt and her head both. Looks like she's hurt in more than one place. Nobody at home over at her sisters', so I brought her to you." Jeremiah panted between words as he handed Tempest off to Micah.

Tempest groaned. The wind had died down. Had she reached her eternity? she wondered. She opened her eyes, and the big white ball had been replaced by porch posts. That was really strange. She'd always thought the Pearly Gates would be fancier, with scroll designs, but they were just big round pillars with banisters between them.

"Go get Elvira, and tell her to hurry," Micah said to Jeremiah as he carried Tempest inside the house.

"Yes, sir." Jeremiah nodded and took off around the house toward Elvira's cabin.

Micah wasted no time getting Tempest upstairs to a guest bedroom, where he gently laid her on the bed. Blood stained her shirt on the left side, some of it dried and some still wet to the touch. It was all over Micah's shirt and hands, but he didn't even notice as he brushed a leaf from her dark hair. A bruise on the right side of her forehead was turning purple, but her breathing was normal. The bruise could have come from a fall from her horse but not the bloody hole in her shirt. It looked more like a gunshot or a knife wound.

Tempest's eyes snapped open, and she frantically scanned the room. She wished she could come back to earth and tell Delia and Fairlee that heaven was a big disappointment. It looked a lot like her bedroom, with a dresser against the far wall, lace curtains on the window, and a piecework quilt on the feather bed. And the preacher had definitely been lying when he said it was a glorious place with no pain. Her shoulder ached something fierce, as if it was on fire.

Before she could form words from thoughts, her eyes fell shut again, and she moaned.

Micah wasn't sure what to do. He couldn't leave her. She might wake up for real and be able to tell him what had happened, but he needed water to bathe her face. Where was Elvira? Surely Tempest wouldn't die before the healer could get there and tend to the wound.

"We can talk," Tempest suddenly said. Her voice was strong, but her brow was furrowed and her eyes tightly closed.

"About what?" he asked.

"You don't have to do this."

"Yes, I do. I had to send for Elvira to tend to you. I can't do it, Tempie. It wouldn't be right," Micah said.

"Delia will hunt you down and kill you if you shoot me," she said as her eyes fluttered open again. "Where am I?" she demanded.

"Jeremiah found you and brought you here. Elvira is coming. She's good at doctoring and a lot closer than going into town for the real doctor," he said.

She could see Constance standing behind Micah. "If I'm fast enough, I can dodge it. Micah, move!"

"Dodge what?" He looked around the room.

She moaned. "Watch the eyes. They'll blink when the trigger . . . Where did the gun go?"

"Where are you, Mister Micah?" Elvira's voice echoed up the staircase in the quiet house.

He stepped to the door. "Up here."

She took the steps two at a time, in spite of her age, and

was breathless when she reached the door. "What happened? Jeremiah said he found her beside a tree. Would have run right past her if he hadn't seen three wolves and thought maybe there was a calf or a colt he needed to see about."

"I don't know what happened, but she's out of her head. There's a knot on her scalp and blood on her shirt. It happened a while ago, because some of the blood is dried," Micah said.

"Well, you get on out of here, because I'm about to take off her clothes. You go find me a nice night shift among your momma's things and hang it on the doorknob. I brought Cherish with me. She's in the kitchen boilin' water. Jeremiah come with us to help however he can. You want him to go for Miss Delia?"

"Not yet. Let's see what's happened first," he said.

"Then get on outta here and let me see about her. Miss Tempie, you be right still, and I'll get this old shirt off easy as I can. We'll see if that arm is broke. I didn't think there was a horse alive that could throw you. I bet if Mister Micah finds the critter tomorrow, he'll shoot it right between the eyes." Elvira talked as she unbuttoned Tempest's shirt.

Cherish carried a bucket of water into the room and filled the pitcher and the bowl on the washstand. Her brown calico dress had two wet splotches on it where she'd sloshed the water on the way up the stairs. "I brought cold water for you to get started. Got some more warmin' on the stove. Jeremiah built a fire, so it'll be hot in no time."

"You stay here and keep the rags wrung out for me," Elvira said to the girl.

Tempest felt soft hands holding her up while another person cut away her shirt with a pair of scissors. When they removed her camisole, she instinctively tried to cover herself, but her left arm wouldn't move.

"Be still, Miss Tempie. I've got to see where you are hurt," Elvira said.

Everything was a confused jumble of sounds and voices to Tempest. People were talking, and she smelled soap. She heard Micah's muffled voice saying something in the hallway. But it all blended together into a strange medley that made her head hurt even worse.

"Oh, my!" Elvira exclaimed, when she'd washed the blood away from Tempest's shoulder and found the hole.

"What is that? I thought she fell off her horse. Jeremiah said that's pro'ly what happened," Cherish said.

"If she fell, it was because she was shot off her horse. I knowed that girl wouldn't just fall off a horse. She could ride anything that she could put a saddle on the back of. Go down to the kitchen and bring me up a good sharp knife and the stirring spoon that's got a long, skinny handle on it. You know which ones I'm talkin' about? And make sure you wash 'em with soap and then stick them in boilin' water," Elvira said.

Micah heard the word *shot* and opened the door. Elvira quickly covered Tempest with the edge of the quilt.

"Do you need whiskey to pour into the wound?" Micah asked.

Elvira nodded.

His footsteps sounded like gunfire on the stairs, and Tempest winced. "Don't shoot," she said, loud and clear.

Elvira rolled her onto her side and scanned her naked back. She could find no holes, but there was a slight bump below her collarbone. "The shootin' is over, Miss Tempest. Now we got to see where that bullet is. Ah, there the little devil is. That'll make it easy to get out. Won't have to cut very far at all. Won't even need the spoon handle to dig around for it."

Cherish carried both items on a tray covered with a clean white cloth. "This all right? Is she goin' to live, or is something hurt inside her?" she asked.

"That'll do fine, but we won't need the spoon. I found the bullet. You'll have to hold her while I make a little hole and get it out, then we'll pour Mister Micah's whiskey onto it. If she ain't passed out plumb cold before we do that, she will be after we do. But it'd take more than this to kill Miss Tempie. She's a tough little woman, just like her sisters. The day that Tyrell and Isaac brought them to River Bend was a day when the angels smiled down from heaven, right along with all four of their parents."

"Tell me what to do," Cherish said.

"And me?" Micah said from the door.

"You give that bottle to Cherish and shut the door. Don't open it no matter what you hear in this room until I tell you to. Miss Tempie will pitch a fit if you see her like this. Now get on out," Elvira said.

Micah shut the door and slid down the wall right beside it.

"Y'all needin' anything else?" Jeremiah called from the bottom of the stairs.

"Come on up here," Micah said.

Jeremiah took the steps three at a clip and waited at the top with worry etched into his face. "Cherish said it was a bullet. Who'd want to shoot Miss Tempest?"

Micah shrugged helplessly. "Might as well sit down, Jeremiah. Elvira said I'm not to come inside no matter what, and I could use the company," Micah said.

Jeremiah sat on the top step and leaned against the railing.

"I figured she'd took a fall off that horse of hers. Didn't see it nowhere about. Guess he run off."

What Sally had said about trading his father's horse came to Micah's mind. Had someone tried to kill Tempest for her horse?

"The horse probably went back to Tyrell's. When they get done in there and can tell me what's going on, I'll go over there and see if he's come home," Micah said.

"You got any notion who'd shoot her?" Jeremiah asked.

"After our Sunday dinner with the Duvals, I sure don't. If this had happened last month, I would have thought maybe she and Constance Duval had a showdown, but they were getting along fine. And I doubt Constance would even own a gun, let alone get the draw on Tempie if there was a battle between them. No one else around here even knows Tempest very well—certainly not well enough to have shot her. She's only been here three months. Maybe it was a stray shot."

"Cherish said the hole wasn't very big. Man shootin' a deer would be usin' a big gun, wouldn't he?" Jeremiah asked.

"Where was she exactly when you found her?" Micah asked.

"You know the path from here to there. At the edge of the trees over there on the right-hand side." Jeremiah gestured with his hands as he explained. "Big old oak tree right there not too far from the path. Just before the pecan trees start. That big one that puts out a shade. Wish I had that tree in my yard to shade the front porch of my cabin. She looked like she'd been sittin' right there and fell over, but she musta crawled there, or someone shot her off her horse."

Tempest moaned so loudly that both men stopped talking and looked at the door.

"Got it. Take that, and give it to Mister Micah. He'll know what to do with it," Elvira said.

The door opened, and Cherish held out her hand with a bullet lying in her palm. Micah took the bloody thing from her and turned it over several times, holding it up to the light. "This looks like it came from one of those new little pistols. We saw some of them over in Greenville at the store around Christmas. Tyrell wanted to buy one for Delia, but she wouldn't have none of it. Said if she pointed a gun at someone, she wanted the gun itself to put the fear of a Lavalle into the person. Nobody would be afraid of something with a two-inch barrel."

Micah was talking too fast but he couldn't stop. "It's too little to come from a rifle, and it's intact, so I don't think it hit any bones. It sure might have come from one of those new Colts I saw."

"Elvira said it went in up under her front collarbone and out below the back one. She don't think it hit nothin' or else Miss Tempest would already be dead. She said to tell you that the bruise on her head is pro'bly what got her knocked out cold, not the hole in her shoulder," Cherish said.

"Cherish, you go down to the kitchen and bring me up the bandage basket," Elvira called out.

Cherish rushed down the stairs and was back within minutes. Micah listened intently but didn't hear any more moans or groans from the bedroom. The next half hour lasted a week past eternity. If Tempest died in that room without one or both of her sisters there, they'd never forgive him. Worse yet, with Tempie's temper, she'd come back and haunt him until his own dying day.

Finally Elvira opened the door. Blood stained the front of her dress, and her face was etched with worry. "She's alive. Don't know how much that thing"—she pointed at the bullet still in Micah's hand—"did to her, but I think she'll mend. Got a bad bump on her head. Looks like she fell or something hit her pretty hard. She's been saying odd things, so it might have done something inside her head. When she wakes up, we'll know. You want me to stay with her while you go for her sisters?"

Micah shook his head. "I'll sit with her through the night. If she's not dying, there's no need to go for them right now. I'll send Ben at first light, and they can stay with her then."

"I don't reckon she ought to be moved for a few days. I'll be back at dawn to make breakfast, and me and Cherish can take turns watchin' after her," Elvira said.

"Thank you, and, Elvira, there's a bolt of calico left in the closet under the stairs. You take it on home with you to-night to make you and Cherish new dresses. Y'all both ruined what you're wearing."

"Thank you, Mister Micah. We'll do just that." Elvira nodded.

Micah pulled a chair up to the edge of the bed. Tempest looked so small lying in the big four-poster bed. The bruise on her temple was turning darker purple, and her hair hung in two long braids down each side of her chest. Elvira must have combed and braided it, because he remembered her having it in a knot at the nape of her neck when they'd talked earlier.

Jeremiah said that she'd been lying in front of the oak tree where they had sat together. That meant there was a possibility that she'd never even gotten onto her horse. If that was the case, then she might have known who shot her. But then, if someone had snuck out of the woods behind her and hit her on the head, then shot her, maybe not. His mind went in circles, going from *what if*s to *how come*s and never reaching an answer.

At dawn Tempest awoke and took in the room without moving her head. Micah was sitting in a chair beside the bed, his head and upper body laid out across the foot of the mattress. Her shoulder throbbed. Her head was a big fuzzy ball of wool.

"Micah?" she rasped.

He jerked awake with a start. "Tempie, what happened?"

"You tell me. Could I have some water, please? And what am I doing here?"

"You were hit on the head and shot in the shoulder and left for dead, and wolves were about to eat you when Jeremiah found you," Micah said.

He poured water from the pitcher on the dresser into a glass. Tempest started to sit up, but the pain in her shoulder said she wouldn't be using that arm to push herself up anytime soon. She groaned. "That hurts like the devil. Is the bullet still in there?"

"No, Elvira took it out." He slipped an arm under her pillow and raised her gently to a sitting position.

"Did it break anything?"

He held the water to her lips. "Elvira says that it didn't. She said it almost went all the way through. Way I figure it is someone was shooting from higher than you were. Maybe standing up and you were still sitting. It went in at a downward angle. You remember who did it or whether they hit you first and shot you second?"

She drank deeply. "I remember wind in my face and someone saying something to sweet Jesus."

"That sounds like what you'd hear and feel when Jeremiah

was running back here with you. Don't you remember anything else?"

She slowly shook her head. "Only telling somebody that we could talk about it. Why would I say that?"

Micah rolled the kinks from his neck. "Probably because you knew whoever shot you and were trying to talk them out of it. You've got a lump on your head. It might take a while or you might never remember. What about your horse? Would he have gone home?"

A flash of memory shot through her mind but was gone in an instant. "Something about selling it. I remember something about selling my horse. I would never sell him. He brought me all the way home from Texas. That was the horse I rode when we left San Antonio."

"You remember all that?" Micah asked.

"Yes, I do. But yesterday? Did this happen yesterday?"

"We were sitting under an oak tree out on the way to the cabin. You were telling me about your mother and father, remember?" Micah was hopeful that if they talked, she would remember.

She slowly shook her head again. "I saddled up and rode away from Delia's. The rest is fuzzy."

Elvira poked her head through the doorway. "Mister Micah?"

"She's awake, but she can't remember what happened," he said.

Elvira crossed the room and laid a hand on Tempest's forehead. "Ain't got no fever. That's a good sign. You get on out of here and let me check things. Go on over to Miss Fairlee's and bring her back with you."

Micah looked at Tempest, who was shaking her head. "Just take me on home to Delia's."

"Miss Tempie, it'd be best if you stayed right here where I can take care of you. Mama Glory don't know doctorin', and neither does Manny. At least stay a couple or three days until that arm starts in to healin'," Elvira said.

"Fairlee and Delia can come and stay or run in and out as often as they want. You are all welcome here," Micah said.

Tempest finally nodded.

"Until we know who tried to kill you, someone needs to be with you all the time. You never know when they might try again. Do you have any idea who would be that mad at you?" Micah raked his fingers through his hair.

"Matthew Cheval, maybe. I helped Isaac kidnap Fairlee from his clutches and then left Louisiana before he could court *me* for the Lavalle money," she said. She'd have people around her no matter which house she stayed in, so what was making Micah so nervous? Combing his hair with his fingers was his classic gesture of frustration.

"Never thought much about Cheval. Sure didn't think of him riding this far for revenge, but if I find that scoundrel on my property, he's bound for a hanging," Micah vowed.

Elvira pointed at the door. "You get on out of here. Cherish is 'bout got breakfast cooked for you, and then you can go get Miss Fairlee. That man comes knockin' on our door, you won't have to hang him. Jeremiah will."

Tempest's grin hurt her head. "Nobody will have to take care of Matthew if he's the culprit who gave me this headache. I'll do it myself."

Chapter Eight

Tempest was tired of the room by noon of the first day. Halfway through the second day she was ready to climb the walls. By day three she was declaring that she'd slide down the banister in her nightdress if they didn't let her do something other than lie in bed.

"I'm going stir-crazy. I can't think that Matthew Cheval is anywhere around, if he ever was, but I can't think of another person who'd want to do harm to me. Please, Fairlee, at least help me get dressed and sit on the porch. I'll take my gun. Rats! I guess I won't. It's on my saddle, and my horse is still missing."

Fairlee shook her head. "Maybe tomorrow. Nobody knows what happened except us and the three here in the house and Benjamin. Micah thinks if we keep it that way, then whoever shot you will raise his ugly head. Either that or you will remember yourself."

Tempest set her jaw and slapped the arm of the rocking chair where she sat. The vibration created pain in her hurt shoulder and her head at the same time. "I hate being cooped up. I don't like living in fear."

"I wouldn't either," Fairlee said.

"We could just go down to the library, and I could sit by the window and read down there. Anything to get out of this room," she begged.

Fairlee nodded. "I don't see a thing wrong with that idea, but you'll have to wear a dressing robe and be very careful. I'm not about to suffer Elvira's wrath, and I would if I caused a problem with that wound. And you are not running around in nothing but a nightdress, even if it does cover you from head to toe."

"Deal," Tempest said. She stood up slowly, and surprisingly, the room didn't spin the way it had when she first slung her legs over the side of the bed the previous day.

Fairlee helped Tempest into the robe and buttoned it all the way down the front. "You will hold tightly on to me. I don't want you to fall down the stairs."

"If I did, I'd take you with me."

Both women turned toward the door at the same time. Before either of them could speak, Micah was blocking the light, his hands on his hips and his expression serious.

"What are you doing?" his deep voice demanded rather than asked.

Tempest's temper flared. "You've got a choice. You can let me go down to the library, or I'm going to jump out that window, steal one of your horses, and go for a ride."

"All right, you win. Jump out the window," Micah said.

Tempest glared at him.

Fairlee giggled. It looked as if her stormy sister had finally met her match.

Tempest turned around and started toward the window.

The floor kept shifting, and the walls billowed in and out, but she'd show him that she could maneuver down a rose trellis just like when she was a kid.

He took two steps and scooped Tempest up in his arms like a new bride. "The library it is, then, but I'm going to take you there and bring you back when you're ready. Elvira would skin me alive if you fell down the steps and broke open her stitches."

Tempest inhaled deeply at the fire his touch created in her heart. She would have liked to lay her head against his chest and listen to his heartbeat, to see if it was doing double time in unison with hers, but she didn't. She could not and would not let a bump on the head cause thoughts that could lead nowhere. Micah had said he'd never trust a woman again, and she believed him.

"I have stitches?" she asked when she could find her voice.

"Elvira says she put a couple in the place where she took the bullet out of your back and three where it went in at the front. Be thankful you were knocked out. She poured whiskey through the wound to clean it."

Tempest shivered. "Maybe that's why I'm dizzy. It has nothing to do with the lump on my head but all that whiskey going straight into my veins."

Micah chuckled. "That was three days ago. I would think the whiskey would be long gone by now. Especially when you take into consideration the meals you've been putting away."

"Are you saying I eat too much?" she asked.

"Well, you don't eat like a bird. Most women I've been around make a big deal out of not eating. You sit right up to the plate and put away enough for a field hand," he said.

"No wonder you don't have a wife. You're as romantic as a cow patty," she smarted off.

"Tempie!" Fairlee chided.

"Well, he is. And don't be thinking that just because you said that about my appetite, it will shame me into eating less. I like food. I work hard and deserve to eat well. You can't insult me, Micah Burnet. I've been insulted by professionals, and you are a rank amateur."

"Well, well," he chuckled. "I guess you are going to live another day to torment the devil out of me."

"Lots of them. You just get ready. By the time I get through tormenting you, you'll be an angel," she said.

"What did I do to you?"

"You do all kinds of things that aggravate me, like breathing."

Fairlee slapped her sister's good arm in a playful gesture. "Tempie! I swear you are as mean as a snake."

"Getting out of that room might sweeten me up," she said.

Elvira met them in the foyer with her hands on her hips. "You be careful with her. That thing starts to bleed again, and I'll have to wash it out with whiskey again."

Micah's smile widened, and the dimple in his chin deepened. "You hear that, Tempie? She means business. And you won't be knocked out this time."

"I'll be good. I promise. I just had to get out of that room. The walls were closing in on me. If it doesn't bleed today, can I ride tomorrow?" she asked.

Micah gently set her down in a rocking chair beside the window so she could see out into the front yard. "Elvira? Can she ride a horse tomorrow?"

Elvira frowned. "She can ride in your buggy in a week if it doesn't bleed. She can ride a horse in two weeks."

Tempie groaned. "By then I won't even remember how to ride."

Fairlee giggled. "Stop whining and be glad you are alive."

A memory flashed and was gone so fast, she barely had time to grasp it. Someone stopped by the tree and dismounted. Someone she knew, and whoever it was talked to her before the gun went off. She'd tried to dodge the bullet but fell, hitting her head on a rock. She remembered the ground smelled funny and she could hear a woman's laughter. *Why would anyone laugh when they'd just shot a person?*

"Tomorrow you do the book work if you feel like it. You didn't get to at the end of the week because of your shoulder," Micah said.

Tempest bristled. "How generous of you."

Micah's gaze locked with hers. "Don't get ugly with me. I'm trying to find something to occupy your mind, since you can't go outside or be seen until we figure out what happened out there in the woods."

Tempest pointed a long, slim finger at him. "Don't take that tone with me. I'll do the book work and be glad for something to keep me busy. I could do more than that. I could ride or go find the sorry culprit who did this. Has my horse shown up yet?"

Micah shook his head but didn't blink. "No, your horse is still out there somewhere, along with your gun and saddle. Isaac went into town and talked to the sheriff, who intends to come out here tomorrow and see if you remember anything by then."

Tempest finally looked away. "I've got an idea. It might bring the shooter out of the woodwork."

"What's that?" Micah propped a hip on the side of the desk.

Fairlee sat down in a comfortable chair next to Tempest. If Tempest had an idea, it probably involved danger, and she intended to put an end to it the minute her sister spit it out.

"Tell everyone that you found my body and it was too ravaged by wolves to have a wake. That you all went ahead and buried me today in that little cemetery out behind the cabin where the late Burnets and Fannins are resting. Go out there and pile some dirt up in a heap, and stick a cross in the ground," Tempest said.

Fairlee's skin crawled. "We can't do that. It's morbid."

"Yes, you can. I bet if you do, then whoever did this will slip up and make a big mistake," Tempest said.

Another flash of memory skittered through her mind, and she could see a sidesaddle in the foggy memory. There must have been a woman with whoever shot her. She could almost picture a bit of lace on the hem of an underskirt.

Micah raked a hand through his hair. "It might work. If Cheval is in the area, he might stop by just to torment Fairlee and Delia."

"If he is, he's got a woman with him," Tempest said.

"Why would you say that?" Fairlee asked.

"I might be getting things all mixed up, but it seems like I can picture a woman being there. I see a gun and a horse, and I can hear a woman laughing. But it might be another day blending in with that one," Tempest said.

Fairlee smoothed the front of her blue dress and frowned. "So you are starting to remember?"

Tempest nodded. "It all started coming back to me last night, but I can't get a handle on anything solid. It's like a memory of Momma will flit through my mind and then one of what happened the day I was shot. It's all confused."

Micah stood up. "I'm not going to tell people you are dead."

"Then simply don't tell them I'm alive. The shooter will go crazy for information. If he's already on his way out West with my horse, I hope it throws him into a river and he drowns."

Fairlee shook her head. "If he's not on his way out of the area, then he might come back and try again. What did you do to make someone want to kill you?"

"Someone as sweet-tempered as me?" Tempest grinned.

Micah stood up and headed out of the room. "On that note, I'm leaving."

"You don't agree?" Tempest asked.

"I'm just getting out of the way for when the lightning comes out of the cloudless sky and strikes you for that lie. The window might deflect it, and it'll hit me," Micah said.

Fairlee poked Tempest on the knee. "You've met your match, girl."

"Not Micah Burnet. I can run circles around him with a bullet hole in my shoulder and a lump on my head. Let's talk about the shooting. Maybe if we go over it a dozen times, I'll pick up something." Tempest had changed the subject because she didn't want to talk about Micah or the way he set her heart to singing every time he walked into the room.

"Okay, start with when you got up in the morning, and tell me everything you remember," Fairlee said.

Tempest drew her eyebrows together. "It was early, and Mama Glory had just fired up the stove. I waited until she had the coffee brewing. We talked about Constance and the way she'd been nice on Sunday. Mama Glory said that she still didn't trust the woman, that she was only being nice to get next to Micah."

She didn't tell Fairlee about the bit of green jealousy that had shot through her at the idea of Micah being with Constance.

"Go on," Fairlee said.

"I poured a cup of coffee and carried it up to my room. I was still wearing my gown and dressing robe, and I stood in front of the window and watched the sun rising. I remember thinking about the trees coming to life and looking less like a bunch of arms and legs flailing about. Then I set the coffee on the vanity and brushed out my hair, got dressed, and heard Etta Ruth cooing down the hallway."

"I want a baby just like her," Fairlee said.

"Maybe you'll be the one who gets the boys."

"Not me. I want three little girls with dark hair like ours."

"And what if you get a dozen boys while you are trying to get those girls?"

"I don't know anything about boys."

"You'll learn."

"I'm not arguing with you about babies today. Tell me more about your day," Fairlee said.

"I finished my coffee, even though it was cold, and went down to the dining room right behind Delia and Etta Ruth. Tyrell was already serving himself off the buffet when I got there. We had eggs and sausage gravy and hot biscuits. I ate strawberry jelly on my biscuit. See? I can remember every detail."

"And then?" Fairlee asked.

"We worked on the garden plans, and Tyrell came in a couple of times. We ate dinner, but he didn't come in for that. Said he was eating at Micah's because they were working over in that area the rest of the day. Then I went for a ride while Delia put Etta Ruth down for a nap."

"Where did you go?"

"To your house."

Fairlee shook her head. "You never showed up there. We

rode over to Delia's in the evening, and I didn't see you anywhere."

"Micah whistled, and my horse stopped," she said.

"What?" Fairlee asked.

"I was going to your house, and Micah whistled. I talked to him, and we hid from Constance."

Fairlee's mouth drew up in a firm line. "Why? I thought you two were on your way to being friends."

"I wouldn't say *friends*. Maybe we're more like two old tomcats that have to share the barn, but there's no love lost between us. Kind of like that," Tempest said.

The next flash brought a picture of Constance getting off the horse and standing over her. Her pulse raced at the vision, and her head started to hurt again.

"What did you talk to Micah about?" Fairlee asked.

"He told me that we talked about Mother and Father. I just remember talking to him and leaning against a tree. My horse was tied to a sapling so he wouldn't wander off," Tempest said.

Delia's voice floated through walls. "Tempest, where are you?"

Fairlee quickly went to the double oak doors and waved at her to join them. "Where's the baby?"

"Manny is bringing her in from the carriage. Has Tempie remembered anything today?" Delia went straight for Tempest's side.

"We've been trying to figure it out all day. I remember the gun and trying to dodge the bullet. I remember hitting my head. Before that I was talking to Micah and leaning against a tree. I'd tied my horse, so he didn't run off. He was stolen—I'm sure of it. He's not out there wandering around with my saddle still on him," Tempest said.

Delia shook her head. "We haven't seen him yet, so he might have been stolen. Whoever did this might have wanted your horse, and you put up a fight. Have you remembered whether it might have been Matthew Cheval?" She touched Tempest's face and held the back of her hand on her forehead. "Still no fever, so that's a good sign. I think you're going to get through this without it killing you."

"Elvira poured pure whiskey through the hole in my chest. Nothing could survive that." Tempest held Delia's hand against her face for a moment before releasing it. Things would be all right. The Lavalle sisters were together. Nothing could penetrate a force like that. Not even Matthew Cheval.

Or Constance Duval, she thought. *Now, why did I think that? Because those were her boots sticking out from the lace petticoat. And because she was riding sidesaddle, and one leg was higher than the other when I looked up. She took her purse off the saddle horn. I should have realized something was wrong then, but I was thinking about Micah Burnet.*

"Are you okay?" Delia asked.

"I'm fine. I could ride a horse and could probably shoot a rabbit. It might smart a little, but I could do it if we were riding like we did from Texas. I wouldn't slow us down a bit," Tempest said. She'd have to think about things a while before she told anyone, to be sure she wasn't mixing up visions from her imagination rather than remembering what had really happened.

"We were going over everything that happened yesterday. I'm going to go get the baby and bring her in here. Manny can go visit with Cherish and Elvira in the kitchen. See if you can jar her memory any better than I did," Fairlee said to Delia.

Delia sat down and smoothed the front of her navy blue skirt. "Keep talking," she said.

"I stopped to talk to Micah. He was leaning against the oak tree and hiding from Constance. He still doesn't trust her. We talked, and that's the end of what I can recollect," Tempest said.

"What did you talk about?"

"Mother and Father and growing up in Louisiana with Aunt Rachel and Uncle Jonathan around."

Delia's face was a picture of worry. "Is that what made you think of Matthew?"

"Maybe. I don't know. It's all right there beyond a thick gray sheet of fog," she answered.

"Think harder. I want you to come home, but the men have gotten together and decided you have to stay here until you can remember, because you could still be in danger," Delia said.

"Why any more at your house or even Fairlee's cabin than here?" Tempest asked.

Etta Ruth was already fussing for her mother, so Fairlee put her into Delia's outstretched hands. She was a plump little girl with Delia's dark hair and blue eyes, but there was a touch of Tyrell in her chin and forehead. She was dressed in a snowy white cotton dress and wrapped in a pink knitted shawl.

"Because our house is on the edge of the property, and so is the cabin. Micah's place is right smack in the middle of the plantation, so someone would have to come a ways onto our land to find you here. It would be easier to get to you at Fairlee's or our place," Delia explained.

But someone like Constance could waltz through the whole place, and no one would suspect her, Tempest thought.

Tempest looked up at Fairlee. "So did you and Constance get the roses planted?"

"We did."

"And?" Delia asked.

"Does there have to be an *and?*" Fairlee answered with a question.

"Your tone said there was," Delia said.

"Okay, then. *And* I'm not so sure about that woman. She wanted to steer the conversation into talking about Tempest, and not in a good way. I was glad to see her leave. I hadn't mentioned it before, but she might have been riding along about the time everything happened. If she saw whoever did it and left you there hurt and dying without stopping to help you, I'd never forgive her."

"Maybe my first impression of her was right all along. What time did she leave your place?" Tempest asked.

"Midafternoon. Said she had to get back to get dressed for supper, that Edith liked them to be all proper for supper even if it was just the three of them."

Tempest smiled. The final piece of the puzzle fell into place. Constance had found her and shot her, stolen her horse, and left Tempest for dead. But she'd have trouble convincing her sisters of a story like that, much less a sheriff. Constance would twist her hanky, spout tears like a raging river in the springtime, and declare that Tempest was her best friend.

Chapter Nine

Tempest had been so glad to see Delia and the baby arriving the next day that she almost shouted. She'd sat on the floor in the parlor and played with Etta Ruth and had even helped set the table for supper. Her left arm was still in a sling, and she had to have help with her hair every morning, but she was becoming more independent with the passing of each day.

Elvira and Cherish served supper in the dining room that evening to all three sisters, Isaac, Micah, and Tyrell. Tempest declared that she was tired of talking about her ordeal, so the conversation went to the next week, when they planned to make a trip into Greenville. The men were going to visit with a cotton buyer from New York, and the ladies were going to use the day to shop.

"By then I can ride in the carriage. Elvira said so," Tempest said.

"But a whole day? It might be too much," Micah said.

"If it is, I can always rest in the carriage, can't I?" The look she shot his way dared him to challenge her. She was rousting ready for a good fight, and if Constance Duval wasn't around so Tempest could snatch her baldheaded, then an argument with Micah would have to do.

"That is a whole week away," Fairlee said.

"By then I'll be completely healed and will be riding every day," Tempest said.

Tyrell chuckled. "They haven't changed a bit since they tossed those nun's habits aside, have they?"

Isaac looked at Fairlee and shook his head. "Did you ever wonder what those Indians did with those habits when they found them in the supply sacks on that horse?"

Micah laughed. "I can still see them riding into battle with those things on their heads for a good-luck symbol."

Tempest's giggle was infectious, and soon all six of them were laughing like schoolchildren let out of a building after a long day of doing difficult numbers.

After supper Tyrell tied his horse to the back of the buggy and drove Delia, Manny, and Etta Ruth home. Isaac did the same and drove Fairlee in the opposite direction. Micah waved until they were out of sight, and Tempest watched from the library window.

The sun was setting like a big orange ball dropping off the edge of the earth when he came inside. He leaned against the doorjamb and looked at her for a long time before she finally realized he was staring, and turned around. In those minutes he realized that he had developed deep feelings for Tempest. He didn't like it, and he'd do his dead-level best to get over it rather than encourage it, but they were there. He cared if she lived or died. He cared if she hurt. He even cared if she was bored to tears because she couldn't go outside.

"Now what?" she asked.

"Tired?"

"A little. Elvira checked the site again this afternoon before supper and said it looked good. I guess the whiskey did its job. I am tired, but mostly I'm antsy. It's as if any moment something is going to jar the fog away and I'm going to see the whole thing crystal clear," she said.

"Did you think of anything else?"

"It's all a jumble. I can't sort out what is real and what might have happened two weeks ago or even a year ago. Maybe another good night's sleep will take care of it. I'm going to take a book up to my room and read until my eyes won't stay open," she said.

"Then you are ready to go upstairs?"

She nodded and started toward him. He met her halfway, scooped her up in his arms for the second time that day, and felt the same sparks dance around the room.

She set her jaw to keep from gasping. The only reason she had an attraction for Micah was because they were the only two left unmarried on the plantation, she told herself. If Sally hadn't died, then Micah would be marrying her, and there would be parties with lots of eligible men for Tempest to flirt with. But Constance had fixed that.

"One more piece to the puzzle," she mumbled.

"What did you say?"

She hadn't meant to speak aloud and had to think quickly. "That I forgot to get a book," she said.

"I'll come back down and get one for you."

"Thank you, Micah, but I could walk up the stairs by myself. My arm is injured, not my legs."

"Elvira says that you still get dizzy when you stand up too fast and that I'm to carry you up and down until she checks you tomorrow. She says that if you fall, you'll likely make your wound bleed, and it might get infected," he said.

When he set her down at her bedroom door, the floor did seem not quite level for a split second, but she quickly got her bearings. "Good night, then."

"Good night. I'll bring a book right up for you."

He disappeared down the stairs, his boots making a loud noise. She heard him fumbling through the books, dropping one and fussing about which one to take. Didn't he know that his deep voice traveled up the stairs? She bit back a giggle and sat down beside the washstand, where the light from the oil lamp came over her shoulder.

When he returned, his breath caught in his chest at the sight of her sitting there in a pale blue dress, with her hair wrapped around her head like a crown and her steely blue eyes looking right at him. She'd been named right; she created a storm in his heart.

She met him halfway across the room and held out her hand. "I appreciate you doing this for me. Oh, I love this story."

"I thought you might. Mother enjoyed it."

He put the book into her hand, but she didn't get a good grasp on it. It started to fall, and she grabbed for it at the same time he did. The book hit the floor with a loud bang, but neither of them heard it. Their hearts were beating too fast, and their eyes were locked in a gaze that sent them both to the depths of the other's soul.

He leaned down slightly. She rolled up onto her tiptoes, and he brushed a kiss across her lips that sent tingles up and down her spine. She wondered if that's what Fairlee felt when Isaac kissed her, or if Tyrell set Delia's ears to hearing sweet bells in the distance.

"I'm sorry." He stepped back.

"Why? I liked it," she said.

"Good Lord, Tempie. That's not a ladylike thing to say."

"And you know very well, Micah Burnet, that I'm not a simpering lady. But it won't happen again, because I refuse to let myself like you as anything other than a friend," she said seriously.

He looked down into her eyes. "Tempie . . ."

She blinked and looked away. "What is it? You don't even like me as a friend?"

He picked up the book and handed it to her. "Nothing. Good night, again, Tempie. Sleep well. I'm just down the hall if you need me."

"You know, this could count as the honest-woman thing. I'm spending nights in your house without a chaperone," she teased.

"We are kin of kin, and you are injured. It's kind of the same thing that Isaac and Fairlee had in the cabin when she was sick."

She smiled and carried the book to her chair. She opened it and read the first chapter but then laid it aside. If Delia or Fairlee had asked her to describe the people she'd just read about, she would have been speechless. The only thing she could think about was Micah Burnet and his kiss.

Finally she blew out the lamp, kicked off her slippers, and got dressed for bed. She draped her dress and petticoat over the back of the rocking chair and snuggled down between freshly ironed clean sheets.

She went over every single detail of the shooting for the hundredth time, down to the look in Constance's eyes when she pulled the trigger. She'd like to string the woman up for stealing her horse. A horse thief was every bit as despicable as a murderer, and Constance had best keep her distance if she wanted to keep all that thick brown hair. Tempest would gladly snatch her baldheaded and scratch out her eyes while she was at it over losing her horse and having her arm in a sling for days on end.

She went to sleep with a dozen ideas of how to punish Constance. They ranged in severity from putting Constance in the root cellar until she owned up to what she'd done, to tying her to the same oak tree, pouring molasses onto her head, and turning a colony of ants loose on her. She figured she'd have nightmares about the woman, but instead her dreams were sweet and took her to the back side of the plantation where a small stream trickled though the land.

Four little boys who looked like miniature copies of Isaac and Micah splashed in the water, getting their clothing all wet. Etta Ruth sat on the bank with her feet in the water and fussed at them when they splashed water on her dress. Delia, Fairlee, and Tempest were putting a picnic lunch on a quilt, and Mama Glory was fussing around, getting things from the wagon.

When Tempest awoke, she was smiling.

Chapter Ten

It couldn't be time to wake up, because she didn't hear Elvira in the kitchen. Tempest had never been one to lie in bed past sunrise. Every day brought something wonderful to do and see, so why waste precious time when she could be up and doing? Her mother had said that her name fit her well; every morning she got up early, and it was as if a storm blew through the house.

But it was the middle of the night. The clock downstairs chimed two times and stopped. It was hours before time to rise, and everything was still pitch-black outside the window. Micah's soft snores floated from his room down the hallway and into hers. She shut her eyes, hoping that she'd pick up the dream about those cute little boys where she'd left off. Seeing the future had been sweet, even if it had been brought on because she'd teased Fairlee about having a yard full of boys.

She heard a strange noise and slowly opened her eyes without moving her head. The hair on her arms stood straight up, and a prickle on her neck signaled danger. A giggle so soft it might have been imaginary reached her ears as she eased the covers back on the bed. She stepped behind the door and peeked out the crack made by shutting it just slightly.

The humming started out very low, and until she saw slender white hands on the banister, she thought perhaps Cherish had come in really early to make something special for breakfast. But those weren't Cherish's hands. They belonged to Constance Duval, and the last time Tempest had seen them, they'd been holding a small pistol aimed at Tempest's heart.

Constance's thick brown hair flowed down her back and looked beautiful against the white cotton robe trimmed in white lace. The moonlight from the window at the end of the landing illuminated her face, giving her an angelic look. But that halo over her head wasn't real. What was it Micah had said? It was a trick of the light.

Constance stopped at the top of the steps, removed her robe, and let it drape down the stairs as if she'd lost it on the way to the bedroom.

Good Lord! What will Elvira think when she comes in tomorrow morning and finds that? Tempest thought.

Then Constance removed her slippers and tossed them down the steps. From the sound, one landed all the way at the bottom and one about halfway down. It would look as if she and Micah had had a rendezvous after Tempest had gone to sleep. No one would believe that Constance had set the stage for a lifetime of misery for poor old Micah. And he had no idea what was going on as he lay in his bed snoring away, probably dreaming of fields of white cotton making the plantation richer that fall.

The thought of what Constance intended for everyone to

think had happened after she'd left half her clothing on the stairs turned Tempest's cheeks brilliant red. Constance was a black widow spider about to pounce.

Tempest touched her own face, and, just as she suspected, it was as hot as if she had fever. If Elvira had been there, she would have dragged out the whiskey and given her a bath in it.

Constance undid several buttons at the top of her gown, showing lots of pure white skin beneath. She cupped a hand over one ear and smiled brightly when Micah snored again. She checked the stairs to make sure all the props were in place and took a step in the direction of his mumbling.

He talks in his sleep. That's another reason I can't be attracted to him, Tempest thought. *But even if he snores and talks in his sleep, I can't let Constance set him up for a lifetime of misery. Being a Burnet, he will do the right thing, no matter what. And, dear Lord, I'd have to put up with her on a daily basis, since she'd be Fairlee's sister-in-law and a cousin by marriage to Delia.*

"You lost or something?" she whispered to Constance as she stepped out onto the landing, careful to keep away from the stairs. Constance wouldn't think twice about pushing her down the steps.

The humming stopped. Had a chicken feather floated down from the ceiling, it would have sounded like a clap of thunder when it hit the hardwood floor, everything was so quiet. Constance turned slowly, eyes wide, hands shaking, and looked at Tempest without blinking.

"You are not there. You are a ghost," Constance whispered.

"What makes you think that?" Tempest grinned, a plan born in the space of a blink of her eyelashes.

"Because you are dead." Constance wrung her hands.

"Oh?" Tempest didn't think it would be laid to her charge if she scared Constance to death. After all, the woman had attempted to murder her.

"I shot you, and there was blood, and now you are haunting me." Constance's voice quavered.

"Did you go back and check for my body? I screamed when the wolves began to eat my flesh. Did you hear me when I cried out for help, to keep them from fighting over my arm as they tore it away from the rest of my body? Tell me, Constance, did you sell my horse for a lot of money? What did you do with my gun?" Tempest asked.

Constance pointed a shaking finger. "I don't have to answer you. You are dead."

Tempest liked playing the part of a ghost. Constance was either hugely superstitious, or her conscience was dealing her misery if she thought she was conversing with a spirit. Tempest didn't care which as long as she gave the woman a scare and made her leave before she woke Micah.

"Yes, I am. You shot me," Tempest said.

"I'm a good shot with my pistol. I got you in the heart. Only Jesus was resurrected. You can't be alive," Constance argued.

"And it took Him three days too," Tempest said.

"That's blasphemy, and you'll go to hell for talking like that," Constance said.

"I expect I'll meet you there, since you murdered two women just to get a plantation."

"If I shut my eyes tightly and count to ten, you will disappear." Constance shut her eyes and put both hands up over them as she did a slow count to ten.

Tempest moved from her doorway to Micah's, being

careful not to touch Constance on the way. To open Micah's door, Constance was going to have to go through her, and even with an injured arm, she had confidence that she could stop her.

When Constance opened her eyes, she inhaled deeply and began humming again. She unfastened another button and looked up to see Tempest standing in front of her.

"Didn't work, did it? Want to know where Sally is, since she's not with me right now?" Tempest asked.

Constance tilted her head up defiantly. "She's dead too."

Tempest smiled. "You should know. You killed her too. Right now she's sitting on the edge of Micah's bed, protecting him from you. You can go on in there, but she's going to be watching you. You want to get into bed with her fiancé with her watching? She knows that you poisoned her by now, so she's not really happy with you."

"That witch. She's ruined everything, and all because she couldn't keep away from Frank." Constance started wringing her hands again.

Micah mumbled something in his sleep. Constance looked past Tempest, then blinked and refocused on Tempest's face again.

Tempest smiled. "I'm still here. Don't plan on going anywhere. Sally and I like this house. If you want to do the honest-woman trick, go on and try. Just remember, both of us live here now, and you'll see us no matter where you look."

Constance pondered on what Tempest said for a full minute. Finally she sighed and picked up her robe. "I hate you," she said.

"Go home to Jackson, Constance. I'll be everywhere you look. I've got free rein of the whole plantation, and I promise I will be everywhere you go. If you go to the outhouse,

I'm going to be waiting by the door when you come out. And if I were you, I'd get rid of that gun, because someday I'm going to figure out a way to tell Micah where to find it and what you did with it."

Constance sighed.

Tempest took a big chance and said, "You want to touch me to make sure I'm a ghost? Maybe you aren't as good a shot as you think."

"You are dead," she said flatly.

"Then go back to Jackson. And before you leave, I want my horse, saddle, and gun to show up at Delia's, or Sally and I will come to haunt you in Jackson. I'd really like to see what kind of husband you end up with." Tempest deliberately caused her voice to quaver.

Constance rushed down the stairs and out the door.

Tempest hurried to the window and watched the woman mount up on a paint horse and ride away, the moonlight illuminating her white nightgown and the white splotches on the horse's flanks.

The next morning Tempest's horse showed up just outside Tyrell's stable, tied to a sapling and feeding on green grass. The saddle was still on the animal, and Tempest's gun was in its sheath.

Chapter Eleven

All morning Micah whistled one minute and frowned the next. Thinking about the way he'd felt with Tempest in his arms when he kissed her made music in his heart. But that stopped when he thought about the awkwardness that would be between them when he went home at noon. Would she be angry at him, or would she simply act as if the kiss had never happened?

He'd worried for nothing, because Tempest was gone when he got home. Washington met him in the foyer with the news.

"Miss Tempest has gone back to Mister Tyrell's house. Elvira begged and begged her to stay another night or two at the least, but she said she was well enough and she was going home. So I took her," Washington said.

Micah touched him on the shoulder. "That's fine. She's right. If her wound was going to make her sick, it would have already done so."

"She said to tell you to come to supper at Mister Tyrell's tonight. That she's got something to tell the whole family, and she's not telling it until everyone is there."

"Did she say what it was?" Micah asked.

"No, sir. That's all she said. Hugged Elvira and Cherish and thanked me for taking her home. Oh, and guess what Miss Delia said when she come out on the porch to see who was drivin' up? She said that Miss Tempest's horse had showed up that morning out by the stables. Wonder where it's been the past two days."

"No telling," Micah said. "Please tell Elvira I'll have dinner in the office. I expect I'll be doing books all afternoon."

"Miss Tempest did the book work early this morning before she left. Told Cherish that next week she'd be riding over here to do the ledgers again. I guess she will, since her horse done come home." Washington smiled.

Micah nodded. "She's that tough, all right. I'll still be having dinner in the office."

"I'll tell Elvira," Washington said.

Micah sat down in the desk chair, laced his fingers behind his neck, and sighed. If Tempie was angry about the kiss, she wouldn't have taken care of the books for him. If she wasn't upset about it, then why did she leave? Elvira and Cherish doted on her even more than Mama Glory would.

His mind went in circles. He ate a thick slab of ham between two pieces of freshly made yeast bread, but didn't taste a single bite while he pondered the questions lying heavily on his heart. And when he finished the last bite, not a single answer had put the questions to rest.

"What does it matter?" he muttered. "It just happened. It wasn't planned, and it has no future."

Tempest declared that she was tired of being mollycoddled when Delia tried to make her lie down and rest the remainder of the day. "My mind is clear, so my brain is fine.

My shoulder will finish healing up in a few days, and then I can hold Etta Ruth again. Right now I just want to go see my horse."

"We couldn't believe it when he turned up at the stables. He looks well fed and none the worse for being gone that long. Doesn't even have saddle sores. It looks as if someone took good care of him and then saddled him up and brought him home. Are you sure you're able to walk that far?" Delia asked.

"Yes, I am. Go with me. It's a lovely day. You can bring Etta Ruth. I promise I won't try to saddle up and ride. I just want to see him and check my things to make sure they are all there," she said.

"All right. I suppose if you get tired we can stop and sit under a shade tree and rest," Delia said.

"No thank you. I'm not sure I'll ever be able to sit under a shade tree without getting spooked again," Tempest said.

"Do you need a shawl?" Delia asked.

"That would be nice. Aren't you going to offer to carry me up and down the stairs like Micah did?" Tempest teased.

"If you are able to walk to the stables to see about your horse, I reckon you're more than capable of getting up to your room and getting your own shawl," Delia answered.

Tempest laughed, but she found out that holding the hem of her skirt up while maneuvering the stairs without holding the banister was a tough job. One arm was still in a sling, so she couldn't hold the railing or her skirt with that hand. She tried, but her shoulder ached.

"Not so easy, is it?" Delia said.

"Oh, hush. Coming back down won't be nearly so hard. I'll be wearing pants."

"Whose?"

Tempest stopped halfway up and growled, "Dang. Elvira took them away. She cut my shirt off and . . . I bet she burned my trousers."

"That's what I would've done with them." Mama Glory joined Delia at the bottom of the staircase.

"May I borrow yours?" Tempest asked Delia.

"No, you can't. She wore them when she went riding with Mister Tyrell to see where it was that you got shot. And they are being washed out in the backyard right now," Mama Glory told her.

"You don't need to wear trousers, anyway. You promised you wouldn't try to ride your horse," Delia reminded her.

Tempest pulled the skirt up and tucked it into the waistband of her pantaloons. "There! That makes it a lot easier."

"I do declare. Your poor old uncle and aunt back where you come from was pro'ly glad to see you go, if you acted like that all the time. Tell me you didn't do that over at Mister Micah's place."

Tempest had the grace to blush, but she didn't tell them that she'd let Micah kiss her or that she'd enjoyed it immensely.

"Dotty, where are you?" Mama Glory yelled.

The young maid came running from the back of the house where she'd been folding linens as they dried out on the lines. She was out of breath and wiping her forehead when she found Mama Glory.

"You get on upstairs and help Miss Tempie. You see to it that she don't do nothin' foolish," Mama Glory said.

Dotty nodded and hurried up the stairs behind Tempest. When they reached the bedroom, she shut the door. "I'm glad you're back home, Miss Tempie. I missed you. Now let's get that dress off and get you into a nightgown. You need to rest after that trip home. Your bed is clean and fresh. I'll bring up your supper tray myself. Is there anything special you want?"

Tempest shook her head. "I'm not going to bed. I'm going down to the stables to see about my horse, and the family is having supper together at the table tonight. Tell Mama Glory we're all six going to be here, so we'll need plenty of food."

"Yes, ma'am," Dotty said dutifully, but it was evident from the stern look on her young face that she didn't agree with a thing that Tempest was about to do.

Tempest picked up her shawl, and Dotty draped it around her shoulders.

"Will my hair hold up for the rest of the day and supper too?" she asked Dotty.

Dotty nodded. "Wind ain't blowin' today. Just a little breeze ever' so often. I expect it will be fine, but if it's not, I'll fix it for you. Don't expect you're much good at doin' it up with that arm in a sling."

"You're right about that. If it doesn't look too bad, we won't bother with it. I don't want to fight with those stairs any more often than I have to," she said.

By habit, when the whole family came to dinner, they sat in the same places: Tyrell at the head of the table, Delia to his right with Fairlee beside her, Isaac at the other end with Micah to his right and Tempest on the other side of him. They'd taken their seats that evening, and Manny lined up the food down the middle of the table. Chicken and dumplings, pork chops cooked with apples, and side dishes of baked sweet potatoes, green beans, and boiled cabbage.

"I heard Elvira wasn't happy with you. She thought you

should have stayed at Micah's until the sling came off your arm." Fairlee looked at Tempest. She wore a lovely pink dress that evening, styled with tucks and tiny buttons all the way down the front. Her dark hair was twisted up on top of her head, and her cheeks were radiant with happiness.

"No, she wasn't happy, but I'm fine. If I'd stayed there much longer, she would have made me an invalid," Tempest said.

She hadn't looked right at Micah since he got there half an hour before. He'd nodded at her, but she'd kept her eyes trained on his mouth instead of his eyes. For one thing, she wondered how that particular set of lips could make her knees go weak. For another, she didn't want to look into his eyes for fear she'd see disgust at her for saying aloud that she wasn't sorry he'd kissed her.

"I understand you have something you want to tell us, Tempie," Isaac said as the platters and bowls were passed from one to the other.

"Yes, I do. It happened last night at Micah's. I was afraid the memories were disconnected parts of more than one puzzle, when they started coming back yesterday. But they were confirmed last night, and even though I can't prove it, because it would be her word against mine, I'll tell you what happened when I was shot. I remember every single thing." She went on to relate the story, detail by detail, leaving out only the part about Micah's father and the kiss she and Micah had shared.

Fairlee laughed so hard that tears rolled down her cheeks. She picked up her white linen napkin and wiped the tears away, but then she got the hiccups. "I think you have gotten your revenge."

"And saved *your* sorry old hide at the same time." Isaac

poked Micah's arm. "What would you have done if you'd awakened this morning with Constance in your bed and her clothes scattered down the stairs?"

Micah turned to Tempest. "I suppose I owe you a big, big thank-you, even though revenge rather than protecting me was at the root of your actions,"

She looked up at the same time Micah looked over at her, and their eyes locked for a split-second before she blinked. In that short time she felt as if he'd kissed her again. She touched her lips to find that they were cool and not nearly as warm as he'd made them feel with his eyes. He'd never know how much protecting him had been at the root of her encounter with Constance. If revenge had been her sole motive, she would have let Constance make it to his bed before she said a word. That would have been far more embarrassing to the woman.

"You're welcome. But if she hadn't already been seeing ghosts brought on by her conscience, she'd never have believed me," Tempest said. "I just played on the demons already in her mind."

Fairlee's eyes widened. "Do you think she's insane? Will she come back for you again when she finds out you're alive?"

"She'd better bring her supper if she does, because it's going to take her all day to get ahead of me the next time. I should have listened to my gut. It kept telling me she wasn't to be trusted," Tempest said.

"None of you are to be running around alone, not even on our land, anymore. You have to take an escort with you until we are sure she goes back to Jackson. If she doesn't, I'm going to have a long talk with Vincent," Tyrell said.

"But . . . ," Tempest started.

Delia raised a palm toward her. "He's right. No arguments. You can ride anywhere, but you've got to have someone with you."

An impish smile played at the corners of Tempest's mouth. "But I'm a ghost. I can walk through walls, and bullets would pass right through me."

"Does your shoulder hurt?" Micah asked.

"Of course," she snapped.

"Then I reckon you aren't a ghost after all. I'll ride with you. Just tell me what time you usually exercise your horse, and I'll be here. I owe you that much for keeping me away from the preacher," he said.

"Two o'clock every afternoon while I put Etta Ruth down for her nap," Delia said.

Tempest shot a look across the table meant to fry her oldest sister on the spot. "I can take care of myself."

"I'll be here at a quarter till," Micah said.

"We'll be looking for you." Delia smiled.

"I'm sitting right here. I can speak for myself," Tempest said.

"Then tell Micah that you won't be riding until the end of next week. Tell him that Washington is going to take you over there on Friday next week to do book work, and so it will be the following Monday before you can ride a horse," Delia said.

Tempest rolled her eyes toward the ceiling. "You heard her. I do get to go to town with the rest of the family tomorrow, don't I, *Mommy?*"

"Don't you take that tone with me. I'm not your mother, but I'm not above a good old fight, and, honey, I will win, since you've got a bum shoulder." Delia's eyes flashed anger.

"Well, look who can still get mad. I thought Tyrell had taken it all out of you," Tempest said.

"Not me. That'll take a lifetime." Tyrell held up his hands defensively.

Isaac looked at his new wife and said, "Amen!"

"You got anything to add to that?" Tempest asked Micah.

"Not me," he said quickly.

Chapter Twelve

Saturday was a beautiful April day. The sun came out brightly, and there was no wind, only a very gentle breeze. The sky was the color of Delia's eyes, a lovely, pale, clear blue without a hint of a cloud anywhere in sight. All the trees were bursting out in shades of minty green, and the birds were singing.

Tempest was almost giddy with the prospect of getting away for a whole day. Shopping for fabric to make new dresses for all three of the sisters plus tiny little summer things for Etta Ruth would be fun. It would be her first trip into Greenville, and even though she would have enjoyed it more if she could have ridden her own horse and gone without a sling, she wasn't complaining one bit.

The men brought up the rear of the coach, and from their tone, Tempest could tell that they were just as excited as the women about going into town for the day. It took a full hour and most of another before Washington parked the carriage in front of the general store. Tyrell opened the door and helped each woman out.

"We're going to the livery to look at a couple of mules," he said. "Then we have a ten o'clock appointment at the bank, and an eleven o'clock one at the hotel café with the cotton buyers for next fall. We'll meet you in the café for lunch at noon," he said.

"We'll be ready by then, I'm sure. And after that?" Delia asked.

"We are at your mercy to carry packages or help hold the baby all afternoon," Tyrell told her.

She smiled up at him. "She gets heavy after a little while. You might be volunteering for a big job."

Even though it would have been highly improper for a husband to kiss his wife right there on the main street of downtown Greenville, the look Tyrell gave Delia was so personal that Tempest felt a little pang of jealousy. She wanted that kind of relationship when and if she ever found a husband.

"We'll get our supplies here first; then after dinner we can make a trip to the milliner and to the cobbler. Tempest says her riding boots need new soles," Delia said.

Tyrell tipped his hat and joined his cousins, who were already on their way across and down the street to the livery.

"Got your list?" Delia asked Fairlee.

"Right here." Fairlee held it up.

"How about you?" Delia asked Tempest.

"Oh, yes. I've looked forward to this day all week. If I didn't write things down, I'd forget something. Do you think they've still got some of those little guns? I'd like to see what I could do with something that has a barrel less than three inches long."

"Tempie!" Fairlee exclaimed.

"Well, I would, and I may buy one. Bet I can outshoot you with it," Tempest teased.

"You can not," Fairlee said, then clamped her hand over her mouth.

"See there? We haven't lost our competitiveness, have we?" Tempest opened the door and stood to one side. "Go on. Age before beauty."

"Brains before ignorance," Fairlee said with a giggle.

Delia rushed inside the doors first. "Mothers before everyone."

"That's not fair. You know how much I want to get a family started," Fairlee said. "I want three little girls just like us."

"You are going to get four little boys. I dreamed it," Tempest said.

The sales clerk came quickly from the back of the store. "Can I help you ladies with something? The fabric shelves are full. We just got a shipment yesterday. And we restocked the whole store last week," she said.

"Well, hello." The preacher's wife, Mary, and his daughter, Martha, stepped out from behind the display of lace and threads.

"Hello to you," Delia said.

"I've made my selections. Maybe I could hold the baby for you." Martha reached out.

Delia put Etta Ruth in her hands. "Thank you."

"Look, Mother, isn't she the cutest thing you've ever seen? I want a little girl just like her someday," Martha said.

Mary put a finger over her lips. "Shh! That's no way for a single girl to be talking in public. Remember you are a preacher's daughter."

Martha blushed. She was almost as tall as her mother and had the same nondescript brown hair, but her eyes were a lovely mossy green and her complexion as pretty as Etta Ruth's.

"I've bought the navy blue serge for new dresses for me and Martha. She's planning to put a white collar on hers with white buttons down the front," Mary said.

"White lace around the collar would be lovely," Tempest said.

Mary shook her head. "Too frivolous for our station in life."

"What do you think of this pink batiste and this fine lace for baby dresses?" Delia asked Martha.

"It's beautiful. She'll look like a doll." Martha hugged the baby tighter.

"My brother-in-law, Tyrell Fannin, said you have some of those new small handguns. I'd like to see them," Tempest told the clerk.

Mary shook her head, the look on her face leaving no doubt how she felt about a woman looking at weapons. Martha winked slyly.

"The guns are back here. Had a little boy whose parents didn't keep a watch on him come in last week. He thought the new guns were toys and had one in each hand, throwing a fit for his father to buy them for him. I put them behind the counter after that," she said, and she turned to Mary. "I've got your purchases ready. Will you be taking them with you, or should I deliver them to the parsonage later today?"

"We'll take them. Martha, give the baby back to Miz Fannin, and we'll be on our way. It was nice to see you ladies," Mary said.

"Likewise," Delia said. "You'll have to come to Sunday dinner sometime soon."

"Thank you, we'd like that." Martha beamed.

"I could like the daughter. She reminds me of us when we had to wear nun's habits," Tempest said.

"How's that?" Fairlee had pulled a bolt of yellow checks from the shelf and was trying to visualize it made up into kitchen curtains for her new house.

"Like she doesn't belong in the skin of a preacher's daughter and would really like to have something different," Tempest said. "I'll look at those guns later, ma'am."

"Whenever you are ready," the clerk said.

"What do you think for the kitchen?" Fairlee asked. "Delia said I can have Mama Glory's daughter, Rosy, every day until I get all my sewing done for the new house. So starting Monday, she's coming to my house, and I want to have things decided and ready."

"Yellow is bright and cheery for the kitchen," Delia said. "I've been thinking about taking down the muslin in my kitchen and brightening it up with red checks."

"Oh, that would be so pretty with red geraniums growing in pots in the windows," Fairlee said.

Time seemed to have wings, and the morning flew by. When it was time to meet the men for dinner, they were barely halfway through their lists, and Delia was jostling a fussy baby on her hip.

"I've got a few more things to look at. Y'all go on, and I'll be right there. I do want to take a peek at a gun. Don't look at me like that, Delia. I won't buy it right now. I want to hold one and think about it first. Maybe I'll come back and buy it before we leave," Tempest said.

"We promised that we'd stay together," Fairlee reminded her.

"It's just across the street. I can see you from here, and I promise I won't be long," Tempest said.

Delia pointed to a bolt of pale pink cotton. "Please add five yards of that to my purchases. I'll be back after we have dinner to pick out trim and embroidery threads to do some handiwork on them. Come on, Fairlee. If Tempie doesn't get finished by the time Micah gets to the café, we'll send him to babysit her."

"Finally!" Tempest said when her sisters were out the door. "Now please let me see those guns."

The clerk retrieved the cutest little weapon she'd ever seen, with its pearl handle and short barrel. "What kind of range does it have?" she asked.

"My husband and I own this store and the livery. He usually has a man who runs the livery for him, but Jonas is down with a fever today, so he's down there. I'm telling you this because I'm not a gun person. Never shot one in my life and barely know how they operate. If you'll come back with your sisters after you have dinner, I'll send someone to get my husband to answer your questions," the clerk said.

"That will be fine. I probably should be going anyway. They'll send the posse after me if I'm not there on time for dinner," Tempest said, laughing.

She still had the gun in her hand when she heard footsteps behind her. It couldn't have been ten minutes yet, but maybe Micah could answer her questions about the gun. When she turned around, Constance Duval was no more than five feet from her.

"Oh!" Constance gasped, her drawstring reticule dangling from her wrist.

"Hello, Miss Duval. What can I do for you today?" the clerk asked.

"I need to buy a stagecoach ticket to Jackson. I understand it leaves in fifteen minutes," Constance said quickly, without taking her eyes off Tempest.

The clerk looked at Tempest. "You won't mind if I go ahead and do that, will you?"

"Not at all." Tempest lowered the gun to her side.

Constance's eyes followed.

"So you aren't dead?" Constance whispered when the clerk went to the back of the store to get a stage ticket.

Tempest moved her finger to the trigger. The gun wasn't loaded, but Constance wouldn't know that for absolute sure. "Doesn't look that way, does it?"

Constance moved past her to the clerk's desk, where she paid for her ticket. When she had it in her hand, she whipped around quickly to be sure that Tempest wasn't a ghost.

"I'm still here," Tempest said.

"Please excuse me. I hear my supply wagon for flour and sugar at the back door," the clerk said as she disappeared behind a curtain.

"I'll swear you are lying if you say a word. You can't prove a thing," Constance hissed.

"I reckon the bullet that Elvira dug out of my back will match those in that gun in your purse, won't it? You just get on that stagecoach and go away, and only my family will ever know," Tempest said. "But remember that I *will* tell if you ever come back here again."

Constance blushed so red that Tempest thought her face would ignite into flames.

"You told Micah!"

Tempest nodded. "I told the whole family. They know about Sally too, so if Edith and Vincent's sons ever come up dead of a strange fever, someone will know to look for you."

"You are a witch!"

"No, just a ghost—or was it a distant relative of Jesus?"

"A blasphemous witch at that. They should burn you at the stake."

"They should hang you from the gallows. Your ride is here," Tempest said, nodding toward the stagecoach pulling up outside. She waited until Constance flounced out of the store, her chin up and her eyes flashing, before she put the gun back on the clerk's counter.

Tempest waited on the wooden sidewalk until Constance's trunk was loaded and the driver had made sure there were no other passengers. She had no doubt that Constance would pull that little pistol from her purse and shoot her dead on the street if she turned her back on her for an instant.

The stage pulled away, leaving a cloud of dust in its wake. Tempest wiped it away from her blue dress and hoped she'd done the right thing. If Constance went on to kill other people, she would never forgive herself. She watched the stage until it was out of sight and took a first step off the sidewalk, only to see Micah coming at her through the fog of dust. Was he just an apparition that would disappear when she blinked her eyes, or was he real?

She blinked.

He didn't disappear but kept coming toward her with a smile on his face.

In a few long strides he was beside her, his arm held out for her to take. She was so glad to see him that she didn't argue. She slipped her arm into his and let him lead her across the street.

"Constance just left on that stage. She knows I'm alive," she whispered.

"Are you all right? Is she in one piece? I need to talk to you alone. We haven't had a moment since you left my house," he said.

"I'm fine. Actually, I'm better than fine. It's over, and I can get on with my life without looking over my shoulder every minute. And Constance is in one piece, unless she exploded because of anger. Tomorrow afternoon by the oak tree?"

He slowed his pace. "Won't that bother you? I mean, it's where she shot you."

Tempest stomped her foot. "It's not the tree's fault. Dang! I can't ride yet, and Delia will never hear of me walking that far alone even if I tell her that Constance left town."

"I'll figure something out. Just be ready at two o'clock," he whispered, as he opened the café door and stood aside to let Tempest enter before him.

He seated her at the table and took his place. "What are we having?"

"I ordered roast beef. Tyrell got ham. Those are the two choices. Both are served with sweet potatoes, carrots, and green beans," Delia said.

The waitress brought a platter of biscuits and an assortment of jelly jars, along with a dish of freshly churned butter, and set it in the middle of the table. She put a saucer, a fork, and a knife beside each guest and asked, "You all want the roast beef or ham? The others have already ordered."

"Tempie?"

"Ham."

"I'll have the same," Micah said.

"Be right out with your plates. Help yourselves to the biscuits while I get it all ready," she said.

Tempest laid one on her saucer and slathered it with butter. "Look. We're all sitting in the exact same places we do at home when the family is together for a meal."

Fairlee took a biscuit and passed the platter on to Isaac. "Old habits."

Tempest smiled. "Habits? Do you reckon our habits are still with our Indian friends?"

That started speculation about their nuns' habits and whether or not the Indians would be scared of holy women's garments or if they thought they'd be good omens in battle.

Tempest ate her biscuit and listened, but her thoughts were elsewhere. Was Micah becoming a habit, like putting on comfortable old shoes? Now that Constance was gone and out of the picture, would their friendship continue to grow, or would it simply die in its sleep? She slid a glance over to him, only to find him staring at her with what looked like the same questions in his eyes.

She quickly blinked, and when she opened her eyes again, she was looking across the table at Delia, who was smiling brightly.

Chapter Thirteen

The preacher was going on and on about forgiveness in the Sunday-morning sermon. A fine spring drizzle fell outside, so there was little chance that Micah would find a way to get Tempest out of the house that afternoon. She'd looked forward to talking to him alone, hoping that they'd sort out the business of that kiss, which had stayed on her mind for days. Ladies didn't talk to men about such things, barely mentioned them to other women, but she and Micah were good friends. Besides, he didn't think she was a lady.

"So there," she mumbled.

Delia poked her leg. "Shh!" she said, and she nodded toward the preacher.

Tempest listened for all of ten seconds before her mind wandered again. Surely God didn't expect her to forgive Constance Duval for shooting her and leaving her for dead. If He did, He was going to be disappointed for a long, long time.

Micah sat at the other end of the Burnet-Fannin pew. If he leaned back, he could see Tempie's profile. She looked pretty that morning in her yellow dress and white lacy shawl. Her arm was still in a sling, and she'd told everyone that she sprained it. Letting people think that she'd been clumsy enough to take a tumble off her horse, hit her head on a rock, and have to be rescued by Washington couldn't have been easy for independent Tempest Lavalle.

He admired her more every day. Last spring she'd been a thorn in his side even if she was untiring on a horse, could shoot the eyes out of a scorpion at twenty yards, and could fry up a rabbit so that it melted in his mouth. Those weren't things that ladies did, and it had aggravated him that a woman as beautiful as Tempest had to act like a man.

When she arrived at Delia's place, she'd still been a burr under his saddle, with her smart mouth and devil-may-care attitude. But since that horrible morning when Sally Duval made her deathbed confession, Tempie had been his friend and confidante. She hadn't betrayed the secret, not even when she spilled the beans about Constance getting caught on her midnight charade.

Not many men would have been as close a friend as that. He stole another look at her. Her profile was perfect. A nice straight nose, big eyes, delicate chin, and full lips that had haunted his dreams since he kissed her.

Good Lord, I'm falling for Tempie! This can't happen. We can be friends, but I vowed to never trust another woman. Not after Sally. Not enough time has elapsed for me to think about another woman, not even under the circumstances.

He sat up straight and attempted to listen to the morning sermon. That the Duval pew was directly in front of him didn't help matters at all. Edith kept dabbing her eyes with a handkerchief, and Micah wondered if she was missing her two nieces. If she knew the truth, she'd be wiping away tears of something other than sorrow.

He was amazed to find that he didn't harbor bitterness anymore. Sally had made a horrible mistake, but it was in the past, done and over. He was glad for the first time that they hadn't caught up to the bandit who'd taken his father's horse. The man would have denied killing Morris Burnet, but no one would have believed a thief's word. He leaned back again and stole one more look at Tempie. It was all because of her that he'd managed to get through the last weeks, even the whole year.

In the beginning, when he and his brother and cousin had first gotten out of that San Antonio jail, he'd had to concentrate on keeping the "Sisters" safe through all the disasters they'd encountered along the trail from Texas to Louisiana, including confronting Santa Anna himself. Then, after the women had shed their habits, he'd had to work hard to keep up with the *Lavalle* sisters. All of it had taken his mind off his father's death. When Sally confessed on her deathbed to killing Micah's father, it had brought on renewed feelings of mourning and despair, not for her but for his father. And Tempest had been there to help him through all of it.

On that trek last year, Delia and Tyrell had made their way back to River Bend a little slower than the others, arriving a week after Isaac and Micah had on horseback. And she'd settled in, bringing Tyrell happiness and a woman's touch to the plantation again. So that had helped. Then Isaac and Fairlee had their "kidnapping" adventure and their own trip back to River Bend. And then there were two women on the plantation that had been set up with two sisters from the beginning: Tyrell's mother and his mother. Only now there were three men and three women on the plantation. Was his fate tied up with Tempie's?

"Amen! Would you please give the benediction, Micah Burnet?" the preacher said in a loud, booming voice.

Everyone stood and bowed their heads. Micah stuttered through a short prayer, and the congregation began to move toward the door, where the preacher waited to shake everyone's hand.

Edith Duval caught Micah at the end of the pew and hugged him tightly. "It's still hard to sit in the pew where Sally sat with us so many Sundays. I can't imagine your pain. We told our cook to make a big dinner today. We would like for you all to join us. I've invited the preacher and his family also, and his daughter plays the piano beautifully, so maybe we could have some afternoon hymns."

"Of course we'll come," Isaac answered for Micah. "Thank you for the invitation."

Micah could have gladly strangled his older brother. There went all his chances of getting Tempest alone for even a few minutes. And he'd been looking forward to talking to her and sorting out this big emotional elephant that was between them every time they were together.

"Why did you do that?" he asked Isaac under his breath when Edith and Vincent had made their way to the door.

"We've excused ourselves twice already for a dinner since Sally passed. It's beginning to be awkward, and they've been our neighbors all our lives. We can't keep avoiding them because you are 'grieving,' " Isaac said.

Micah stood back and let Isaac and Fairlee go ahead of him, then Tyrell and Delia. When Tempest stepped out into the aisle, he took his place beside her. "We'll be having dinner at the Duvals'," he whispered.

"When did that happen?" she asked.

"Just now. Edith asked, and Isaac accepted. It seems we can't avoid them forever. And the preacher and his family are joining us. Their daughter plays the piano, so we'll be hearing from her this afternoon," Micah said out of the corner of his mouth.

"What are you two whispering about?" Delia asked.

Lately her sister Tempie and Micah had formed a friendship that she wouldn't have believed was possible. But then, if someone had told her the day that they rode up to the front of the San Antonio jail in a wagon and dressed in nuns' habits that she'd be married to the best-looking outlaw in the group within a month, she'd have had that person declared insane.

"We're going to dinner over at the Duvals'. Isaac accepted for us all," Tempest said.

"Well, that will be nice. I'd given Mama Glory and Cherish the day off with their families, so we were just going to have cold cuts for dinner. I'm sure Tyrell would rather have a good hot meal, and Edith has been eager to get her hands on the baby so she can have some play time with her. I suppose she's lonely since Constance left. You be careful what you say, Tempie," Delia said seriously.

"I'd rather go home to cold cuts. Can Washington drop you all off and take me home? I feel a headache coming on," Tempest said.

Delia shook her head emphatically. "You've never had a headache in your life except when you got a bump last week, and that's over and done with."

Tempest sighed. "It's recurring right now. It feels as if I might even have nausea with it."

"You never could fake being sick. We are going, and so are you." Delia looked from her sister to Micah.

"But all afternoon with nothing to do but listen to piano music?" Tempest whined.

"It won't hurt you to sit still."

"How do you know? It might kill me, and you'll have to wear black for a whole year. Have you ever seen a baby in black? All those pretty colors we bought for her summer dresses will go to waste. Are you sure you want me to go?"

"If it kills you, we'll bury you, and I'll tell everyone that you made me promise to wear red to the funeral," Delia said.

Micah chuckled, and Tempest turned on him. "I'm not bailing you out if the preacher's daughter bats her eyes at you. Remember, you are now an eligible bachelor, and the women will come flocking around you like hens after a worm."

Delia blushed. "Tempie Lavalle! That's crude talk for a lady."

"It's the truth," she protested, but she snapped her mouth shut. She'd almost said that she wouldn't bail him out of trouble *again*. That would have brought on a whole raft of questions that she couldn't answer.

It was a tight fit for six of them and a baby inside the carriage, but just as they'd done at the dinner table, they took their usual seats after shaking hands with the preacher. Tyrell, Delia, and Tempest on one side; Isaac, Fairlee, and Micah on the other.

"You look like you could explode," Fairlee said to Tempest.

"I don't want to go to the Duvals'. I want to go home. Delia is being bossy and making me go," she pouted.

"It'll be fun. Which reminds me. Our house is going to be ready to move into in a couple of weeks. I'd like to have a party, but it shouldn't be a big affair since . . . well, you know. So what do you think of just us and the Duvals on a Sunday afternoon?" Fairlee asked.

"I think that would be wonderful," Delia said. "It would repay them for today. Maybe by fall enough time will have elapsed that we can go ahead with an autumn harvest party like we had last year, don't you think, Tyrell?"

"That's up to Micah," he answered.

"Of course we can have the harvest party. We've had it on River Bend our whole lives. Life goes on. You girls didn't wear black and carry on for a year after your parents passed, and neither did we. So, yes, we will have the party," Micah said.

"Good, we'll start planning for it. It'll give us something cheery to look forward to," Delia said.

"What all is involved?" Fairlee asked.

"It's just like our fall ball back in Louisiana. All the neighbors come for the whole day on a Saturday. Food is set up in the dining room and the tables kept full. The children play games on the lawn, and the men gather in the library or on the porch. It gives the ladies a chance at some women talk, and then in the evening there's a big ball out in the backyard. I'd love to have the flower garden at least in some kind of order for it this year," Delia answered.

Tempest bit back a moan. That would mean that women would be flitting around Micah even worse than a bunch of clucking hens after the early-morning worm. And what was so crude about that saying anyway? If that's the way they acted, then it was the truth.

For the first time she admitted to herself that she didn't want other women looking at Micah, flirting with him, or even talking to him. She was jealous, and that made her even madder than figuring out that she'd let herself be duped into getting shot—by a woman, no less. Had it been a big, burly man, the embarrassment wouldn't have been nearly so great. But being bested by another woman was bitter medicine to swallow.

The Duval house rose up from an immaculate lawn like a big white mountain against a pale blue sky. It was twice the size of Tyrell or Micah's house or the one that Isaac was building for Fairlee. The windows had been thrown open to allow the spring breeze to flow through the house, and lace curtains billowed inside. The preacher's family had arrived before the Burnets and Fannins and were being escorted into the house.

"Ever wish you'd made plans for a bigger place?" Delia asked Fairlee as they got out of their coach.

"No. I want to be able to find Isaac when I want him. I like things small and cozy. I could probably live in the cabin for the rest of my life," she said.

"I don't expect a dozen mean little boys would do well stacked up like cordwood in that little cabin," Tempest said.

"I told you, I wouldn't know what to do with boys. I'm having all girls," Fairlee whispered.

"You are getting four boys. At least, that's what I dreamed the other night," Tempest said.

"Those were *your* boys," Delia teased.

"Not hardly. I'd have to have . . ."

"You'd have to have what?" Micah asked.

Fairlee and Delia both laughed.

Tempest blushed. Dang it all, anyway. Her face had turned crimson more in the past three months than it had in her whole life total. "Nothing. I dreamed that Fairlee had four little boys, and now they're trying to pawn them off on me."

"And what would be wrong with four little boys? There

were three of us growing up, and we'd have gladly liked more," Micah said.

"Just think of all the fun Etta Ruth would have with a bunch of little boys to lord over," Tyrell said.

"I'll take all of them," Isaac said.

"Good afternoon," Vincent Duval greeted them at the door. "We are so glad y'all could come over. Edith has been blue since Constance left yesterday. We'd thought she'd make her home here, but she received a letter from her mother and was called back to Jackson in a hurry. She wouldn't even let Edith go with her to catch the stage, because she said it would be too painful for both of them."

Tempest didn't tell Vincent that if Constance had stayed, it would have been far more painful, even unto death. "I saw her at the station. She seemed eager to get back to Jackson. I hope nothing was wrong."

"No, she just said that her mother was lonely for her, and, since Sally had passed, that she was sad and she'd be better content in Jackson. Truth is, I really think she missed the excitement of a bigger place," Vincent whispered behind his hand. "If you men would like to join me in the library for a spot of coffee before dinner, we'll let the ladies go to the parlor where Edith and the others are waiting. I know Edith is eager to play with the baby. She loves our grandchildren but only sees them a couple of times a year, since the boys live in Vicksburg."

Tempest followed Delia and Fairlee into the parlor. Edith was holding court from a chair at the end of the settee. She wore a black silk dress with a pearl broach shaped like a flower above her heart. The preacher's wife wore subdued navy blue cut with a high neckline and a billowing full skirt devoid of any kind of trim. She was a tall woman with sharp angles to her face and mousy graying hair, but her blue eyes were bright and her smile genuine. Her husband was her opposite. Shorter by several inches than his wife, he had a round bald head with a rim of gray hair, thick gray eyebrows, and a baby face. His brown eyes and smile were both staid and serious all the time.

"Hello, ladies. Bring that baby on in here for us to admire," Edith said.

"I do love babies, especially little girls that you can dress up in frills," Mary, the preacher's wife, said.

"Did you dress me in frills?" Martha asked.

She was shorter than her mother and had the same mousy brown hair, but her eyes were a lovely dark green, and she'd been blessed with her father's round face. She was slightly overweight, and her dark blue shirtwaist pulled at the buttons. She would have been lovely dressed in a bright yellow dress with a dipping neckline to accent her lovely bosom, but if a preacher's daughter couldn't even have lace on her collar, then she sure wouldn't be allowed to have a stylish dress with a low-cut neckline.

"No, you didn't have frills. Your father thought they were too frivolous," Mary said.

"Well, I do not intend to marry a preacher, and when I have a little girl, she's going to wear lace and frills," Martha said.

"Oh?" Edith cut her eyes around at Martha. "Is there a wedding in the near future?"

Martha's round cheeks turned scarlet. "Not that I know about."

Dinner was called before anyone could press the girl for further information. When they were seated, Tempest found herself between Martha and Micah. Evidently Edith didn't think it would be proper for Micah to sit beside someone who wasn't related or at least shirttail kin.

Micah and Vincent discussed the price of feeding hogs and calves for the winter food supply on the plantation, but Micah had trouble keeping his mind on the conversation. He kept trying to fabricate an excuse so he and Tempest could leave early that afternoon, but nothing feasible would come to mind.

"I understand that you had quite the adventure last year when you returned from Texas. Would you tell us about it?" Martha asked.

"Delia, tell her about the baby we found," Fairlee said.

"You tell it, Tempie. It was your baby for a day and night before we found those good folks to take her in," Delia said.

Micah had almost forgotten about the orphaned infant, but the whole story came back to him in a flash. The way Tempest had taken care of the little girl and kept her close had proved that she would make a good mother, even if all she had were ornery boys.

Tempest laid her fork down. "We rode up on a farm, and the house and barn were burned to the ground and still smoking. Only a cow and a few hogs were left alive. The place looked and smelled awful. We heard later that some evil men were robbing and looting and making things look as if the Indians were on the rampage. We never really found out if it was an Indian attack or those men, but the woman who lived there had been killed. She'd wrapped herself around her baby to protect it, and the little girl was still alive. Fairlee said that we could take the cow with us, so the little thing would have something to nourish it."

"I remember thinking that the cow would slow us down

several miles a day, but Delia said that we should milk the cow and take as much as we could with us, then stop along the way and buy milk from farmers," Tyrell said.

"Well, we couldn't leave the baby alone to die, but we sure couldn't have a cow trailing along behind us," Delia said.

Tempest went on. "I milked the cow while Fairlee took care of the baby and the men buried the woman. And then we were back on the road, with nary a sign of the man of the house. But he hadn't come out of the woods or in from a pasture, so we figured he must have been killed in the fire.

"The baby was so good. She must have been fed not long before we got there, because she slept really well. I guess the ride was like a cradle and kept rocking her to sleep."

"How old was she?" Martha asked.

"We figured a couple of months. She wasn't much bigger than Etta Ruth is now," Tempest answered.

"How long did you have her?"

"That day and night and all the next day. Then we came to a farm where we hoped to buy milk. The couple who lived there were Betsy and Thomas Cunningham. They couldn't have children of their own and fell in love with the baby. We talked about it and decided to let them have her. It was a hard decision, and we were sad for days. They named her Rosetta Lavalle Cunningham after our mother," Tempest said.

"So that's where you got the name Etta for your baby," Martha said.

"And Ruth is Tyrell's mother's middle name. She was Amelia Ruth Fannin," Delia said.

"It's a sweet name," Martha said.

"I always liked good, solid, biblical names like Mary and Martha, Thomas and Mark. Martha would have been named Thomas if she'd been a boy," the preacher said.

"Doubting Thomas?" Martha asked.

"Martha!" Mary said.

Tempest turned in her chair and said, "Well, I'm glad you are Martha instead of Thomas."

"Me too," Martha said through clenched teeth.

The conversation went back to cotton and the price the farmers hoped to get for it that fall.

"Who is he?" Tempest whispered to Martha.

"Who is who?" Martha looked just beyond Tempest, as if afraid to look her in the eye.

"You know. Who is the fellow you are in love with?"

"He's not a preacher," Martha answered from behind her napkin.

"Does he come to church?"

Martha shook her head. "That's why it's so difficult to see him. That and the fact that Father doesn't like him."

"Why?"

Martha shrugged.

"Do you love him?"

"Oh, yes, and Father will too, when he gets to know him. He's just got a sore spot when it comes to Irishmen."

"Is it Ben?" Tempest guessed.

Martha nodded.

Tempest smiled.

Dinner was over after a scrumptious apple cobbler was served with clotted cream sprinkled with cinnamon. The ladies retired to the parlor again, and the men headed to the library.

The rain had stopped, and the sun was shining brightly. Tempest couldn't sit still. She roamed from one end of the parlor to the other, looking at the trinkets on the mantel and the doilies on the tables and chair backs.

"Martha, other than the trip to town when we saw you and your mother, I've been pretty cooped up. Would you like to go for a carriage ride with me?" she finally asked.

"We were going to ask her to play the piano," Edith said.

"Not on Sunday. Her father would never hear of that. Not even hymns," Mary said.

Tempest could have kissed the woman right on the cheek. "Maybe we'll have Washington drive us over to River Bend just for some fresh air. I'm used to riding every day, and since I hurt my arm I've been stuck in the house. I'm sure Martha and I would enjoy the outing."

"You can't go without an escort," Delia said.

"Why? We'll be in a closed carriage, and Washington will be driving," Tempest argued.

Delia shook her head, and Mary did the same.

"It wouldn't look right. Two young women out without an escort," Mary said. "I suppose I could go with you."

"We could ask Micah if he'd agree to go with us," Tempest sighed.

Delia nodded. "If he'll go with you, then I think an outing with Martha would be a fine thing." She grinned at Martha and said, "She gets testy, though, when she's around Micah. You might wish you hadn't agreed to go with her, Martha."

"Mother, are you sure you don't mind?" Martha asked.

"Just be back by four. We'll have to get home in time for a light supper and Sunday-night prayer meeting," Mary said.

"Is that ample time?" Martha asked Tempest.

"Oh, yes," Tempest said. "Two hours should give us plenty of time to drive through River Bend and back."

Chapter Fourteen

"That was pretty sneaky," Micah said.

"Yes, it was." Tempest nodded.

Martha and Ben were sitting beneath the same old oak tree where Constance had shot Tempest. Plenty of light shone between them, but their arms were stretched out and their fingers entwined as they talked, in tones so soft that they didn't even carry on the soft afternoon breeze.

"How did you know?" Micah asked. "Ben never even told me who he was interested in, and you found out in one afternoon."

"I was a nun for a week. That gave me divine powers," she teased.

"Okay, holy woman, tell me the future. Are we going to be friends?" Micah asked.

"I suppose we already are that. I never would have believed it possible, but you saved my life, so now I guess we've got to be friends," she said.

"Elvira saved your life. And Jeremiah might have had a

hand in it. I didn't do much of that lifesaving stuff," Micah said.

"Well, then, I guess we can't be friends," she teased.

"But you do know my secrets," Micah was quick to say. "We've shared everything ever since Sally died. So that not only makes us friends but best friends. Don't little kids in the schoolyard say that about the friends they tell secrets to?"

"I did. Only most of the time I was telling my secrets to my sisters," Tempest said. Was this flirting? There was a gleam in Micah's eye that she hadn't noticed before. Maybe spring fever was contagious, and the wind had carried it from Ben right up Micah's nose. She sat back on the carriage seat and decided that she liked flirting, even though it seemed a heck of a lot scarier than looking down the barrel of that little gun Constance pulled from her purse.

She heard a loud snore and jumped to peek out the window. Surely Ben hadn't fallen asleep. Not when he had a few precious moments alone with Martha. The noise had barely died down when it started again.

Micah grinned. "It's Washington. He's fallen asleep up there in the driver's seat."

"I need some fresh air. Want to walk for a few minutes?" Tempest asked.

He opened the carriage door, stepped out, and extended his hand. "Five minutes up toward Isaac's place and five back, and then we'll have to get back to the Duvals'. Or else Martha will be late, and there will be problems."

She braced herself for the warmth of his touch. Sure enough, when he let go of her fingers, both her cheeks and her hand felt hot.

He walked beside her, their hands brushing, but he made

no effort to lace his fingers through hers, even though she longed for him to do so. Still, she told herself, their friendship had been born of a secret and then thrived as they stuck together through adversity. It could easily be one of those things that required drama to survive and would die out in simple normalcy.

She was glad that Elvira had finally pronounced her arm strong enough that she could toss the sling that had curtailed her riding and movement for two whole weeks. It still smarted if she tried to lift anything heavy, but at least she could ride again. She hoped that nothing ever happened to make her be dependent upon everyone else again.

"Why would the preacher be against Martha and Ben courting?" she asked.

"Ben is a fine man, but he's Irish and the foreman of a plantation. He's never gone to church much," Micah said.

"Oh?"

"His dad was Catholic, and he had to go all the way into Greenville. He tried to go on Easter and Christmas. Ben does the same."

"Oh, my!" Tempest said when understanding dawned.

"Martha's been raised Protestant by a zealous father. She's an only child born later in her parents' life, and she's been taught to do her father's will from birth. That she's even talking to Ben against her father's wishes surprises me. She's not a strong woman like you Lavalle sisters," Micah said.

"Don't be too quick to judge. She might fool you," Tempest said.

"If she stands up to the preacher, I will be fooled. Did Edith mention Constance?" Micah changed the subject.

"Just said that she had to leave. I hope we didn't set her loose to hurt someone else," Tempest said.

A rabbit darted across the path in front of them. "Remember the morning that Delia had rabbit frying for breakfast, and Tyrell said he hadn't even heard a shot fired?"

Tempest smiled. They'd shared a lot, the angels and the outlaws. "And we let him know right quick that we didn't waste ammunition when a knife would work just as well."

"You think Martha could throw a knife and kill that rabbit?" Micah asked.

"I think if she truly loves Ben, she can do whatever it takes to nurture that love. If she doesn't, then he didn't need her anyway," Tempest said.

"Time to turn around and go back. You going to play matchmaker very often, or is this a one-time thing?"

She swept around and kept in step with him on their way back to the carriage. Even at that distance she would swear she could still hear Washington snoring. "I'm not playing matchmaker. We took a ride through River Bend for something to do this afternoon. I didn't tell Ben to be riding along this path at this time. I haven't even talked to him in a week. All I did was ask Martha if she'd like to go for a ride. Fate did the rest."

"I think even fate would be afraid to mess with a Lavalle woman," Micah said.

"That's a point we could argue all day. If that were the truth, then why wasn't fate there protecting me when Constance pulled that gun out and shot me?"

"In five years you may know the answer to that," Micah answered.

"Why five years?"

"That's what Mama Glory says. When something would go wrong in our lives, she'd tell us to think about it in five years and see if it hadn't happened for a good reason," Micah said.

"Fanny used to say the same thing, only she said in three years."

Ben and Martha were standing close together beside the carriage when Tempest and Micah arrived. He was close enough that he could whisper, but there was still space between their bodies. Her face was flushed and her eyes bright. His smile was wide, and when he looked at Martha, love was written on his face.

He tipped his hat and helped her into the coach. "It was a pleasure for our paths to cross today."

"Yes, it was," Martha said.

Ben stepped aside. "Thank you, but how did you find out?" he asked Micah.

"Don't thank me. It was Tempest. She's got divine powers," Micah said with a chuckle.

"Well, tell her not to lose them." Ben laughed.

"You've got what?" Martha asked Tempest, as she settled into the seat beside her.

"I was teasing Micah."

"Thank you for this. Ben has asked me to marry him," Martha said.

Tempest twirled around in her seat. "Ben did what? Have I survived a . . . fall from my horse, only to die at the preacher's hands?"

Martha giggled. "He wouldn't kill you outright, but he might attempt to preach you to death."

"That could be worse than death by a bullet or a noose," Tempest admitted, laughing. "So what did you tell Ben? Are you going to think about it for a while and then give him your answer?"

"Answer to what?" Micah asked.

"Ben asked me to marry him," Martha said proudly.

Micah raised an eyebrow.

"And I said yes. He'll have to talk to you about my coming to live in his cabin, and I'll have to talk to my parents. I think he's getting the easier task," Martha said.

"Me too." Tempest shuddered.

"Ben is a grown man. He doesn't need my permission to take a wife," Micah said.

"And I don't need my father's permission to marry, but I'd like to have it, just like Benjamin would like to have your blessing, since he works for you," Martha said.

"What about your differences in religion? And when did all this get started anyway?"

Martha smiled. "Scripture says that love is patient and conquers all things. I believe that. And we met at a social last spring at the Duvals'. Father doesn't approve of dancing, so Ben sat under a tree with me. Said he had two left feet and didn't dance. I think he was just saying that. Whoever heard of an Irishman without music in his feet and soul?"

Micah nodded. "Ben can dance."

"Maybe he'll teach me sometime after we get married," Martha said quietly.

"I'm sure he will," Tempest said.

The preacher and his wife were ready to leave when they arrived back at the Duval house. Martha barely had time to thank Edith for the lovely dinner before her parents hustled her off to their wagon.

"We are ready to leave also. We were all waiting for you to return," Delia said. "Edith, darlin', thank you for a lovely afternoon. You and Vincent will have to come over to River Bend in the next few weeks for Sunday dinner. Did I tell you that Fairlee's house is nearly done and we plan on a small Sunday-afternoon gathering to celebrate when they are moved in? We'll let you know the exact date and time. We're hoping for the first week in June. That way it won't be too hot, and if the weather is pretty, the children can play on the lawn. Fairlee's been working very hard to get the grass growing."

"It will take a few years to make it look as nice as yours," Fairlee said.

Edith smiled. "Don't expect it to look like my yard right at first. I've been working on this place for over thirty years."

"Well, mine won't ever be this pretty, but maybe you can give me some tips when you see the place," Fairlee said.

"Are we ready?" Tyrell asked.

The ladies all hugged Edith one more time before they got into the carriage.

Fairlee and Delia shot Tempest a look.

"What did I do?" she asked. "We just took a turn around the plantation. We weren't gone that long."

Fairlee nudged her sister with her shoulder. "Two hours didn't seem so long when you left, but after an hour we ran out of things to talk about. Edith had started to yawn and could barely keep her eyes open. Mary wanted to be gracious and leave, but Martha was still gone. We'd about decided that we'd all go home and Washington would bring her and the preacher back to the parsonage when you drove up. I doubt Edith will be inviting us for dinner again next week. If she does, Isaac and I get to take Martha for a ride, and you have to stay behind."

Isaac covered a yawn with the back of his hand. "If she does, you'd better not accept."

"I wouldn't want to be a mouse in the corner when she lowers the boom." Tempest grinned.

"What boom? The one I was ready to lower onto you? I was ready to go home an hour ago," Tyrell said.

"Well, we've got some news that will make your eyes open up really wide," Tempest said.

Micah kicked her foot. "It could be a secret."

"I doubt it. She's about to bust with the news. She won't be able to hold it in until morning. Reckon we'll see fire coming from the east?"

Delia looked from one to the other. "What are you talking about? *Who* are you talking about?"

"Ben asked Martha to marry him," Micah said.

Tyrell laughed aloud. "So that's who the mystery is about. The preacher isn't going to like that news one bit."

"Think he'll put a stop to it?" Isaac asked.

"He'll try," Tyrell said.

"We still in agreement if he doesn't get the job done?" Micah asked.

It was the women's turn to look at the men with quizzical expressions.

"Tyrell?" Delia asked.

"We've been talking about things among us. Ben is a hard-working man, and we thought we'd give him the cabin when he gets married. It's twice the size of his and in a better location," Tyrell said.

Tempest clapped her hands. "What a wonderful idea."

Fairlee smiled. "I can think of no one I'd rather have living that close to me than Martha. Do you really think she'll say something to her parents tonight?"

"I don't know, but I wouldn't be surprised," Tempest said.

Delia and Tyrell had left Etta Ruth sleeping in her cradle and taken a turn around the gardens at dusk that Sunday evening. The window was open into their bedroom, and Tempest was sitting on the porch, one ear listening for the baby's cries should she awaken, the other listening to the last sounds of birds singing before they went to roost. She heard the horse before she saw it coming down the lane, with two riders on it. It wasn't trotting but taking its time, and as it drew nearer, she could make out two voices: one soft and feminine, the other deep and masculine.

She left her rocking chair and went to stand on the steps. "Martha?" she asked when she could make out the riders.

"We've got a favor to ask. A big one," Martha said as Ben helped her slide from his arms to the ground.

"Her father didn't take too kindly to me askin' for her hand." Ben dismounted and slipped an arm around her waist. "I went to the parsonage and was waiting when they arrived. The preacher wouldn't let me into his house, so we talked out on the porch. I respectfully asked. He loudly declined."

"I was afraid of that. I'm glad you were there with her," Tempest said.

"We need a place for Martha to stay until we can get married. It'll only be a couple of days, but we want to do this the right way," Ben said.

Tempest nodded. "Of course she can stay here."

"If I do, my father might not want you in his church anymore," Martha said. "He was very angry and said that I had to choose between them and Ben right then. If I chose Ben, I wasn't welcome in their home or in their church."

"What did I ever do to make him that mad?" Ben raked his fingers through his hair the way Micah did when he was frustrated or angry.

"Hello," Delia said from the side of the porch.

"Ben. Martha," Tyrell said.

"Ben talked to the preacher, and he made Martha choose. Now she needs a place to stay until they can arrange a wedding. I said she could stay here. Is that all right?" Tempest asked.

"Of course it is," Tyrell answered.

"Thank you all. I'm afraid I've come just as I am. Father said if I chose Ben over them, Ben had to take me just as I was and I couldn't have any of my things," Martha said softly.

"I don't reckon that's a problem either, is it, Delia?" Tyrell said.

"Not at all. Come on inside, and we'll get you set up in a bedroom. When do you and Ben want to get married?" Delia asked.

"Ben?" Martha looked up at him.

"That's up to you, darlin'."

"Tomorrow if it can be arranged. The day after if it can't," Martha said.

"Then tomorrow it will be. I'll ride into town tomorrow and bring a preacher out here. We'll have a wedding after supper in the parlor like we did when Isaac and Fairlee got married. Mama Glory can make one of those cakes, and I'm sure you girls can find something for Martha to wear," Tyrell said.

Ben smiled. "I can't thank you enough."

"Her dad will come around," Delia said. "It might take a year or two, but he'll finally miss his daughter and see that he got a good, hardworking man for a son-in-law."

"I wouldn't hold my breath," Martha said. "Mother might come around, but it'll take a miracle to make my father change his mind."

"Miracles have been known to happen on River Bend," Tempest said.

"Yes, I guess they have." Martha stood on tiptoe and kissed Ben on the cheek. "I'll see you tomorrow evening. Don't you be thinkin' you'll see me before the wedding. That's sure to bring bad luck, and we need all the good luck we can get."

"Darlin' "—Ben hugged her tightly—"we have all the luck of the Irish on our side."

"And we'll need it," Martha said.

Chapter Fifteen

Micah stood beside Ben, who was so nervous that he stumbled over the words the reverend told him to repeat. Tempest stood beside Martha, who smiled up at Ben and repeated her vows in a strong voice. They cut the cake Mama Glory had made that morning, and everyone in the house, including Mama Glory, Manny, and Elvira, had a piece to celebrate the marriage. Mama Glory put what was left on a platter, and sent it home with the newlyweds in the wagon with the trunk of clothing the sisters had gathered up for a makeshift trousseau for Martha.

Mama Glory had fussed under her breath all day, that the preacher and his wife had done a sorry deed to make their daughter choose between the man she loved and them. No parents who were of any account at all would do such a thing. And then to make her leave their home with only the clothing on her back. Why, there wasn't a servant on the plantation who'd do such a thing, and him a preacher man at that. It was enough to make her want to say words the good Lord would strike her down dead for even thinking.

Tempest and Micah stayed on the porch long after Isaac and Fairlee had gone home and Tyrell and Delia had gone up to their room. Following a day of preparations and excitement, Tempest was both breathless and restless. The morning had started off with the three Lavalle sisters digging in their closets, plus going through trunks in the attic, to outfit Martha with a trousseau. The trunk that had been loaded onto Ben's wagon held undergarments, day dresses, two nice Sunday dresses, aprons, petticoats, and even bonnets. Martha had worn the same wedding dress Fairlee had worn the day she married Isaac. It was a little shorter on Martha but still reached the ground. They'd woven wildflowers together and made a crown for her dark hair, which Tempest dressed high on her head in a mountain of curls.

Martha's last words before she walked down the stairs to Ben's waiting arms was that she'd never felt so pretty in her entire life.

Tempest sighed deeply.

"What was that all about?" Micah asked. "Wishing you were a bride?"

"Gracious, no! Wishing that Martha's mother would have stood up to her overbearing husband and been a part of her daughter's happiness today. She will always regret that she wasn't here, and Martha will always wish she had been," Tempest said.

"Will you be sad on your wedding day that your mother can't be there?" Micah asked.

"Yes, I will. But it's different. My mother would be here no matter who I decided to marry, and if I didn't decide to ever marry, she would support me in that decision also. She and our father raised us to be independent, to speak our mind and make our own decisions. She also raised us to be responsible enough to take credit for our accomplishments and own up to our mistakes. So she'd be here even if I was marrying an Irishman of a different religion than I was, and she'd give me her blessing. How about you? Will you wish your father could have seen you as happy as Ben was today? I bet Isaac wishes your father could have met Fairlee."

Micah grinned. "My father would have loved the Lavalles. Mother was independent like you girls."

"Did you tell Ben about the cabin?" Tempest asked.

"Yes, we did. He's saving the news as a surprise for Martha later tonight," Micah said.

"Was he happy about it?"

"Well, he was born in the cabin where he lives. There's lots of memories there. But he was happy to have a bigger place for him and Martha to raise a family. He suggested we turn his cabin over to Jeremiah and Cherish. It's closer to the big house, and they both have jobs there," Micah said.

"That's sweet of him."

A full moon hung in the sky that night, with only a few wispy clouds moving across it occasionally. She wondered if that was an omen of things to come for Ben and Martha. A bright lifetime with only a few moments of dimness until they settled their differences.

Crickets and tree frogs were in competition for center stage with their singing. A hoot owl joined the mix with a soliloquy beneath the moon and stars. A lonesome old coyote in the distance set up a howl, and the owl hooted even louder.

"I can't see Martha ever letting her own daughter get married without her being there," Tempest said.

"Or Ben either," Micah whispered.

He was so close that his breath was warm on her neck, creating tingles up and down her arms and spine. She turned quickly to find herself wrapped in his arms and his mouth coming closer and closer.

When his lips touched hers, her knees went all soft, as if their very bones had melted. She willed herself not to swoon. Lavalle women didn't succumb to such foolishness, and she wasn't about to be the first.

"Who do I talk to if I want to court you?" he asked when his lips left hers.

"I expect you ask me, Mr. Burnet, but I'd advise you to wait a while longer. Your fiancée hasn't been gone long enough for you to be courting another woman yet," Tempest said breathlessly.

Did she want Micah to court her?

Her heart was singing, *yes, yes, yes*. Her mind was running so hard in the opposite direction that she couldn't have caught it if she was riding her horse at full speed.

"So when would be an appropriate time to ask you such a thing?" Micah asked.

"I wouldn't know. Maybe you've just got marriage fever. Tyrell and Delia still have the bloom on their marriage. Isaac and Fairlee have only been married a few months, and now Ben and Martha. Maybe we'd best give ourselves lots and lots of time before we do something we'll regret," she said.

"Probably so. Well, good night, Tempie. We're getting into that time of year when we'll be working from daybreak until dark, so I won't be around much on Fridays when you come do the books. It's really not such a good time for Ben to be getting married, but fate didn't ask us about that. I understand there's to be a small house party in three weeks. I hope things slow down by then," Micah said.

"I'll visit Martha and include her in things here to keep her from going stir-crazy," Tempest said.

Micah kissed her on the forehead and disappeared toward the stables to get his horse. She touched her lips and then her forehead, but neither were as feverishly hot as she'd expected.

The days barely had enough hours for any of the family to accomplish what needed to be done the rest of the week. By Friday when it was time to go to Micah's to do the books, Tempest was eager to get away to the solitude of numbers and his office.

She kept expecting him to show up all afternoon, but he didn't. Not that Friday or the next, and he didn't come to dinner all week either. When she got to his house on the third Friday, she had a thousand things to tell him. The garden was coming along beautifully. The rose cuttings that Constance had set out had all died, but Mama Glory had brought some from Delia's, and they were growing very well. Etta Ruth was cutting her first teeth at only three and a half months old.

But again Micah didn't show up. Tempest was so frustrated when she left that she decided it was probably best that he did keep his distance. Her words would scorch the hair off his eyebrows and burn his eyeballs, she was so angry with him. She rode home the long way past Martha and Ben's cabin and found Martha taking clothes in from the lines in the backyard. Tempest slid off her horse and tied him to the porch railing.

"Hello! Come in and I'll make us a cup of tea. I've got a cinnamon cake I made yesterday. We'll have a piece. What brings you to this part of the farm today?" Martha asked.

"I just finished the book work for the week and wasn't ready to go home. I'd love a cup of tea. Want some help with those?"

"I've got a good handle on them. Just open the door for me," Martha said. She was dressed in a yellow calico dress printed with dark green leaves the same color as her eyes.

"How do you like it here?" Tempest asked.

"I didn't realize I could be so happy." Martha laid the clothes on the bed, set up beside the fireplace in one corner of the big room. "Isn't this place beautiful? Ben says this is where his parents slept, and the children all had the loft. Boys on one side and girls on the other. I expect it was wall-to-wall kids when they were all home. Doesn't that sound wonderful? I can almost hear the laughter and fighting. Only children miss that kind of family."

"Are you looking forward to having the bigger place when Isaac and Fairlee move?"

"Oh, yes! I really am. I told Ben this is our honeymoon house, and then it can be Jeremiah and Cherish's honeymoon place. But we'll raise our kids in a home"—she blushed and went on—"that has a bedroom with a door. And I'll have a great big yard to plant flowers and a bigger vegetable garden in. Fairlee already put in the garden, and we're going to share it this year. Next year we'll each have our own."

"The attic at Delia's is full, so if you need anything when you get ready to move, please tell us," Tempest said.

"You've done too much already. I feel so pretty in these bright colors, and Ben tells me I'm his bonnie lass."

"You are my friend, and as friends we can certainly share stuff we aren't even using," Tempest said.

"We did make a connection the first time we talked, didn't we? I saw you in church and was in awe of all I'd heard about you. Wearing those trousers and being able to shoot a gun and ride a horse without a sidesaddle like you do. I admired you so much, and then in the store that day, it was like we understood each other without words."

"That's right, and if you need anything, a friend would help," Tempest reminded her. "I noticed the curtains in the cabin are pretty worn. What is your favorite color? We'll make new ones."

"Red. I was never allowed to have anything red, and I love it. The color of a cardinal," Martha said.

"Well, how about that? Delia bought too much red-checked material for her kitchen, and had Dotty take at least a quarter of a bolt up to the attic when she finished making her new curtains. I'll have Washington bring it over tomorrow morning."

Martha clapped her hands. "My life is so full, I feel like I'm going to explode."

Tempest smiled. She wished her life was that full and that something as simple as red curtains could bring her such joy. Of course, she knew it wasn't the fabric but the fact that Martha and Ben were together and in love that made everything brighter and more beautiful.

Chapter Sixteen

Four weeks had gone by since Tempest had seen either Isaac or Micah. She'd only seen Tyrell if she happened to be up very early or very late. Delia was out of sorts because her husband had been spending too many hours away from her, and she declared that, come Sunday, the family would gather for a picnic at the edge of the creek. She'd accept no excuses or reasons other than a hard, pouring rain, and if that happened, then the family would gather at her house. And the men would not go to the library after dinner, and Ben and Martha were coming too, and she wasn't taking no for an answer from anyone.

Tempest teased her all week that even God was afraid to send rain for the crops, because He might get on Delia's bad side. Sunday morning dawned bright and beautiful, no clouds in the nice blue sky and barely enough wind to be called a breeze. Mama Glory had packed a picnic of fried chicken, cheese, and loaves of fresh bread along with fried pies that they could eat with their hands. In another basket she had washrags and towels and enough plates and glasses for everyone. And she had set two gallons of sweet tea in a wooden crate, with special orders that Jeremiah had best drive slowly and not break the jars.

Washington drove the carriage with the women inside, and Jeremiah took a wagon with the supplies. Isaac, Micah, and Tyrell rode on ahead and had the quilts spread out under a willow tree beside the water when they arrived. Ben and Martha were already there, and she'd brought cinnamon cake, baked sweet potatoes, and raisin cookies.

"We'll be back to gather y'all up 'bout suppertime. We'll just keep the coach and wagon at our place if that's agreeable. We can let the horses graze out behind our cabins," Washington said.

"That sounds good. Jeremiah, if you want to take Cherish for a drive in the wagon this afternoon, that would be fine. Horses won't need to be undone that way," Tyrell said.

"Thank you!" Jeremiah beamed.

Tempest sought out Micah the minute she was out of the carriage. His face was drawn, his eyes tired, and he kept combing his hair with his fingers, which was a sure sign he was frustrated or angry.

Micah chose a spot next to the base of a willow tree. When Tempest stepped out of the coach in her peach-colored cotton dress with a wide, sweeping skirt, his mouth went dry. He'd been busy with the spring planting and working from daybreak to past dark, but he could have taken a few minutes on Fridays to run into the house and see her. He'd deliberately stayed away, hoping that the old adage about out-of-sight, out-of-mind would work.

It had not.

He'd missed her. Dreamed about her nearly every night. And every other thought through the day was about her. All he had to do was shut his eyes, and there she'd be in those abominable trousers that he didn't even mind anymore.

And the whole four weeks had proved nothing except that the old saying was false and that he'd fallen in love with Tempest Lavalle. He had no doubt that she'd laugh at him when he told her, but he had to get it off his chest, or it was going to be the death of him. But first he had to take care of another matter standing between him and Tempest, and he planned to see to that before the day ended.

Tempest nodded at Micah and smiled. Even though he looked worn out, he was the most handsome man at the picnic. Even Ben, with the bloom of new love on his face, couldn't hold a candle to Micah. She'd been miserable for the whole month without him in her life. She realized that he'd been working hard, but today he was going to hear what she had to say, come the devil or high water. She wasn't so sure that she could put her feelings into words, but she'd find a way, because she wouldn't know a moment's peace until she did.

"What now?" Fairlee asked.

"This is my wife's party." Tyrell grinned.

"If that's the case, we eat now. I'm starving," Delia said.

"Y'all go to church this morning?" Martha asked.

"I know the Good Book says we shouldn't work on Sunday, and we do give the servants the day off most of the time, but during this season it's all-hands-on-deck seven days a week. In a few weeks things will slow down, and we'll have time for church," Tyrell said.

"We were wondering if it would be a problem if we went to the little chapel . . ." Martha hesitated.

"You talkin' about the one that Mama Glory and Elvira go to on Sunday? The one where Washington preaches?" Isaac asked.

Martha nodded. "I miss going to church, and Ben said he goes there sometimes when he's not too busy. It's not his church, and it's not mine, but it could be ours. I reckon God's word is good in any place."

"Y'all ask Washington about that?" Fairlee asked.

"He said we'd all be right welcome to come hear him on Sunday morning, and there was plenty of room," Martha said.

"Well, then, that's up to you," Delia said. "Tyrell, you ever been to that church?'

"Lots of times. We grew up with Jeremiah, and if our folks were busy on Sunday, we'd go with him. You want to go there? It's a lot closer than going into Greenville on Sunday morning," he said.

"Sure. I'd love to take Etta Ruth and go next week," Delia said.

"Get ready for Mama Glory to pop you on the back of your head if you don't listen," Isaac said with a laugh.

"And there's no pews, just benches without backs," Micah said from his spot under the tree.

"And Washington can't read, so he preaches from memory," Tyrell said.

"Memory?" Martha asked.

"Elvira can read. My mother taught her, and she reads the Bible to Washington. She's tried to teach him to read himself, but he just can't get the hang of the words. He can remember and quote what she reads to him, though, word for word," Micah said.

"Do they have nighttime services?" Martha asked.

"No, just Sunday morning," Tyrell answered.

Martha laced her fingers in Ben's big hand. "I'd like to go next Sunday."

He leaned forward and brushed a kiss on her cheek. "Then

we'll go. I always did enjoy hearing Washington talk when I was a kid and went with Jeremiah. It's more like he's teaching than preaching."

"Me too, but right now let's eat. I've been craving fried chicken all week," Fairlee said.

Delia took plates and glasses from a basket and set them on the pallet. "Y'all are on your own from this point, but if Fairlee is hungry for chicken, you'd better grab some while there's some to get. She likes her chicken, and she's not bashful, so her plate will look like a pen for chicken bones before she gets finished."

"She's telling the gospel truth. Dive in or don't whine later because it's all gone. Maybe we'll serve fried chicken next Saturday evening at our house party," Fairlee said.

"You are moving in this week?" Martha asked.

"Wednesday. The house is finished. I'm stealing Jeremiah for the next three days to tote things from Delia's attic and Tyrell's barn. We stored my things and Tempest's stuff in his barn, and Delia said we could clean out the attic if we wanted. You want to help us decide tomorrow and Tuesday?" Fairlee asked Martha.

"I would love to," Martha said.

"You are a sneaky one, Delia Fannin," Tyrell said, laughing.

She raised an eyebrow.

"You're getting the attic cleaned and not lifting a finger."

"We Lavalles are a crafty lot," she admitted with a smile.

"You are welcome to come clean out my attic too," Micah said. "It's got even more junk in it than what's at Tyrell's place. I bet you could almost outfit your whole house right out of my attic if you wanted to."

"Hey, don't be stealing my help," Delia said.

"There's bedsteads and trunks and more than one vanity,

with the mirrors all covered in dust. If you're going to help, Tempie, you might want to wear your trousers. It's dusty and dirty up there, and skirt hems would get filthy," he said.

"I'll bring a pair for you, Martha," Tempest said.

Martha looked at Ben, who laughed. "Make her wear them home. I want to see that sight."

"Really?" Martha asked.

"Oh, yes!" he said with a wicked gleam in his eye.

She blushed scarlet and giggled. "This will be so much fun. Maybe we can leave a few things in our old house for Jeremiah and Cherish."

Micah finished loading his plate and carried it back to his spot under the willow. Isaac and Fairlee shared a quilt with Ben and Martha, right next to the one where Tyrell and Delia had put Etta Ruth down for her afternoon nap. Tempest put a chicken leg, a sweet potato, and a chunk of cheese onto her plate and carried it to the tree.

"Haven't seen you in a month," she said as she sat down next to Micah.

"Been busy. Isn't that the reason Delia fixed up this picnic? She hasn't seen Tyrell either, and I understand that if Fairlee hadn't been up to her neck in sewing for the new house, she'd be pretty upset with Isaac too," Micah told her.

"You serious about us raiding your attic for stuff to outfit the house and the cabin for Ben and Martha?"

"If it was your house, wouldn't you let people clean out stuff you weren't using?" he asked cautiously.

"I'd be like Delia and feel like I was getting free help," she agreed with a smile.

"Then bring Jeremiah and take whatever you want. It's all going to waste up there in that hot space anyway. I've decided to tell Isaac and Tyrell about Sally today," he said bluntly.

She had a piece of cheese halfway to her open mouth and stopped dead. She snapped her mouth shut and laid the cheese down on her plate. "Why now?"

"I need to get it off my chest. It's May, and it's been almost four months. I've had time to think about it and realize it all happened for a reason. If we hadn't gone off on that trip, chasing down the horse thief, neither of them would be as happy today as they are," he said. He wished he was as content as Isaac and Tyrell, but he was absolutely miserable.

"Okay, but Delia said the menfolk couldn't gather in one spot and talk crops, that we all had to stay together today," she said.

"Then they'll all hear it at once."

"Even Ben?"

"He took care of the whole place while we went on that wild goose chase. He loved my father, and my father loved and respected him," Micah said. "I would have told him anyway, so, yes, Ben too."

"Well, at least let them all get their dinner eaten first. If you spoil Fairlee's chicken, she'll pout for a week, and we're going to have to work together for the next three days," Tempest said.

Micah smiled brightly for the first time that day. Living with Tempie wouldn't be an easy job, but it sure wouldn't be boring or lack passion. The woman fought with passion, loved with passion, and probably would go to her death with passion in her soul. She would keep him on his toes, and they'd fight, but the making up would be well worth every minute of it. He'd finally found what Tyrell and Isaac had in their lives and was scared out of his mind to tell Tempie, for fear she didn't feel the same.

The dishes were put away when Micah and Tempest sat

down on the quilt with Tyrell and Delia. Tempest felt every emotion in Micah's heart and soul, and held her breath for him when he cleared his throat. He raked his hands through his hair, and she pushed back strands that had come loose from the bun at the nape of her neck. He looked at his family and friends and drew his dark eyebrows down. She did the same.

"I've got something to tell you all," he said.

"Well, thank goodness. Ever since Sally died, you've not acted right," Ben said.

"That's when it started, all right," Micah said.

"Well, spit it out," Tyrell said.

"Y'all remember that morning. They sent someone to tell me to come over to the Duvals' because Sally had taken a turn for the worse. Well, she wanted to make a deathbed confession to me, and I had to get it all settled in my mind before I could say anything to you all. It was my fault, and I am so sorry for almost bringing her into the family."

"What he's sorry for is ever letting that woman sucker him. Now you tell them the rest," Tempest prompted Micah.

"Tempie!" Fairlee said.

Micah put up his palms. "She's right. Don't fuss at her." He went on to tell the whole story, from the time Sally confessed to when Constance shot Tempest and told her about poisoning Sally.

Even the birds seemed to have stopped singing, and the whole universe was silent for a long, pregnant minute after Micah finished. "Well, that's it. I'm the cause of both our father's death and Tempest's getting shot."

"You are not," Tempest said. "You can't carry that burden, because it's not yours to carry. It was Sally's, and it is Constance's."

"She's right," Isaac said. "And although it makes me angry at Sally, I have a wife I wouldn't have had if things hadn't worked out the way they did."

"And so do I," Tyrell said.

Ben shrugged. "I'm glad I didn't know about any of it until now. If I'd known your dad's killer was right next door those months you were gone, I would have felt honor bound to take care of matters for you."

"I'm glad you all feel that way about it," Micah said. "And now you know what's been bothering me. It wasn't grief over Sally but anger at first. And then it was grief for our father and then anger again for Constance's part in the whole thing."

"Do you think Edith and Vincent should be warned?" Martha asked.

"I told Constance that she could never come back here or I'd tell them," Tempest said.

"If she does, you will have to," Fairlee said seriously.

"I was over at the Duvals' yesterday evening to take some seed to Vincent. He said they'd had word that Constance had met a New York man on the stagecoach back to Jackson. He owns a fancy jewelry store in the big city and was recently widowed. He's twenty years older than she is, but she eloped with him. I don't think we'll ever hear from her again," Ben said.

"That's wonderful news! Now let's talk about tomorrow and put all this behind us. Fairlee, you've got the bedroom stuff in your cabin for one room in your new house. Are you putting in two beds or just one in each of the other bedrooms?" Tempest said.

"Two, so I can have more company and more kids," Fairlee said, laughing.

Tempest stole a look at Micah while the women talked about the attic raiding and the menfolk shut their eyes to steal a little nap with Etta Ruth. His face had softened, and he wasn't messing with his hair. He actually looked as if someone had lifted a boulder from his shoulders and tossed it into the creek.

She hoped when she cornered him in the next few days and told him exactly what was on her mind that the worried look didn't set up shop on his face again.

Chapter Seventeen

Surprisingly enough, Micah was in and out of the house several times on Tuesday when the four women came to raid his attic. At the end of the day, Jeremiah had taken two wagons with sideboards loaded to the top to Fairlee's new house. Martha, Fairlee, and Delia had ridden over in a second, smaller wagon loaded with beds and vanities, with Fairlee driving it. Tempest had stayed behind to look through the last half of the attic and set anything aside that she thought might be useful.

She was all the way in a back corner, pulling out a small oak table that would fit well beside Ben's chair in the living area of the cabin, when she felt a presence behind her. She very slowly looked around, thinking it was probably a rat. There were two things that Tempest absolutely hated, and rats were both of them. Snakes weren't as fierce as a dumb old rat. Heck, not even Constance with a gun was as scary as a rat.

"Got a little dirt on your nose," Micah said, grinning.

"I thought you were a rat," she said.

"That any way to talk to the man who's giving away his furniture today?" he asked.

"I hate rats, and they seem to like attics," she told him.

"Well, I'm not a rat, and you are one dirty lady."

"Yes, I am, but Martha is smiling, and Fairlee is singing, and life is good today. Dirt washes off. Even Cherish has been helping clean everything all up. Were you aware that she and Jeremiah plan to marry next Saturday night and move into Ben's old cabin? We've been passing some things on down to them. I think everyone on the place has spring fever." Tempest backed up and sat down on the top of an old steamer trunk.

"What about you?" Micah asked.

"What about me?" Tempest shot back. It was the first time she'd been alone with Micah since the picnic. She'd practiced her speech a dozen times a day since then, but now that she had him to herself, she was tongue-tied.

"Do you have spring fever? Would you like to be fixing up your own house?" Micah asked.

"What are you asking? I expect, since the family knows about Sally now, that you could court me," she said.

Micah shook his head. "I'm not asking for permission to court you, Tempie."

Her heart fell. She'd let her opportunity pass, and now it was gone. He'd found someone else to court while he was waiting for her to tell him when the time was right.

"I see," she said.

"I don't think you do. I don't know when it happened, but it did. I've been trying to catch you alone all day because I'm tired of waiting to tell you. I miss being able to talk to you every day and share my day with you, Tempie. I miss our bantering, but most of all I miss this. . . ." He knelt before her and put a fist under her chin to tilt it up for a kiss.

"I miss the way that makes me feel," he said.

"Me too," she whispered.

"Tempest Lavalle, will you marry me?" He spit the words out so fast that she wasn't sure she'd heard him right.

"Yes, I will," she said without hesitation. If she hadn't heard him correctly, she'd worry about it later. "I don't know when it happened either, but I fell in love with you too. Do we have to wait until next winter?"

"Heck, no! I was thinking maybe this Saturday, right here in this house. That way my mother and father could kind of be here with us," he said.

She melted deeper into his arms. "I'd like that. Then on Sunday we can go to Fairlee's new house for the party, and Martha and Ben will have a new home, Jeremiah and Cherish will be in theirs, and I'll have spent my first night in ours with you."

He kissed her again and held her tightly. "This isn't exactly how I planned to do this, but I couldn't get a minute alone with you, and I was afraid I'd lose my nerve."

"I'll always remember that you loved me even with dirt on my nose and wearing my britches," she teased.

"Yes, I do, to both and forever," he said. "Even though I know what I'm seeing in the dust motes above your head is a trick of the light, I'll always remember it as a halo on my angel the day she agreed to be the wife of this old outlaw."

"Darlin', I never was an angel, light or no light, but I'll be very happy to be Tempie Burnet for the rest of my life," she whispered, and she sealed her vow with another long, lingering kiss.